Fallen Angels:

Stories Inspired by the Urban Homeless

By Keith Madsen

Fallen Angels: Stories Inspired by the Urban Homeless

This book is a work of fiction. Any references to historical events, real people, or places are fictitious. Other names, characters, places, and events are products of the author's imagination, and any resemblance to actual events or places or persons, living or dead, is entirely coincidental.

Jacket design by Ava Wood

Manufactured in the United States of America

ISBN: 978-1-965142-47-9 (Paperback)

ISBN: 978-1-965142-48-6 (Hardback)

Library of Congress Control Number: 2025908192

This book is dedicated to the volunteers across this country who give of their time and compassion to care for the needs of the unhoused men, women, and children seeking a secure home.

Contents

About the Stories

These stories are based on street people I met while serving on the pastoral staff of the First Baptist Church of Portland, Oregon, from 1998 to 2006. The church had a feeding ministry to the homeless and the poor people who lived in some of the decrepit apartments in the downtown area. Over three hundred people would be provided a hot, substantial meal twice a week, and as staff liaison to this ministry I would often help serve and then visit with the people while they ate. My approach was not to raise any spiritual issues myself, as I did not want it to appear like some kind of "spiritual confession" was a cost of the meal. However, many shared their stories with me, and I listened.

Most people in the United States and Canada have become acutely aware of the problem of homelessness. The conditions which cause this phenomenon—low wages, mental health issues, and high cost of rent—are most prominent in urban areas and are not limited to one part of the country. I have been a pastor in the small city of Bellingham, Washington, as well as in the medium-sized city of Topeka, Kansas; the large metropolitan area of Seattle; the population dense state of New Jersey; as well as the medium-sized city of Wenatchee, Washington, where I now reside and work. Homelessness was pervasive in each of those places.

Some people think that homelessness is caused almost entirely by alcohol and drug use, and certainly in some cases that is a factor. But among the homeless you can also find many other factors. According to the United States Interagency Council on Homelessness,

"While there are many drivers of modern-day homelessness, it is largely the result of failed policies; severely underfunded programs that have led to affordable housing shortages; wages that do not keep up with rising rents and housing costs; inadequate safety nets; inequitable access to quality health care (including mental health care), education, and economic opportunity; and mass incarceration. In effect, more than half of Americans live paycheck to paycheck and one crisis away from homelessness."[1]

By sharing the following short stories, I am hoping to help readers to see homeless people as *people*, people who are in some respect just like them. There is a tendency among some in political power to typecast the homeless, and especially those who are immigrants, as "the other"—as dangerous threats to society. That's why I hope that in these stories you just see people.

These stories, however, are fictional. They do not violate the confidences of any of the people with whom I talked, and none of these stories portray actual life events. I did meet a woman who claimed to have been a stand-in for Judy Garland (as in **"The Body Double"**), and that she had held Liza Minelli on her lap when Judy Garland's daughter was an infant. I never discovered whether or not her story was true, and none of the other events portrayed reflect what I knew of her story.

I did visit on several occasions with a Native American man with one leg, as in **"Thunder Rolling Down the Mountain."** His name was Roy. But the story I have assigned to him is out of my imagination. He was found dead in an alley one night.

I also met many homeless teens fleeing domestic abuse, teens who used street names and congregated in street families, as in **"Getting Lost."** They seldom wanted to give their real name, and fleeing abuse at home was a very common reason for their presence on the street.

Latinx immigrants, like Maria in **"Getting Lost"** and **"In a Foreign Land,"** abounded, and one never knew whether or not they were in the country legally or illegally.

I met several homeless people who spent most of their waking hours in the county library, located across the street from the church where I served on the pastoral staff. Some of them were among the best-read people I have known, and I met several who wrote poetry. But again, the story of Mister Yeats in **"The Top of the World"** is fictional.

There was indeed an old woman with cataracts who begged on the streets and who few people could resist donating to, as in **"The Emergency,"** but I knew nothing of her real story.

As in any city, there were prostitutes around, and I knew a church that invited them in to get acquainted with them as people, as in **"The Invitation."** There are more progressive churches across the country who have taken initiatives in this kind of way, in line with the way Jesus associated with "prostitutes and sinners." Even Christian writer and sociologist Tony Campolo spoke of having a late-night birthday party for a prostitute and invited other prostitutes. I'm sure it would be a controversial, high-risk venture for most churches.

There was also a woman who came to the church who walked through the streets of Portland pulling two shopping carts full of her belongings, which she vigilantly defended, as in **"Taking Inventory."** She did indeed frequently take inventory of her belongings, and she had some things most people would not see much purpose for. Even though she was often out of touch with reality, she played flawless classical piano. I enjoyed listening to her play on several occasions.

Of course, the streets were full of vets with PTSD, as in **"The Mission."** While veterans organizations and hospitals do what they can, the ghosts of war can be very persistent.

Alcohol and drug abuse drags many down into the streets, of course. But while many want to be judgmental about that, saying things like, "They brought it upon themselves," I still go with the old saying, "There, but for the grace of God go I." For a couple of years, I taught young people about the dangers of opioids, and I know how they can take over a person's brain and turn them into another person. Oftentimes people who get hooked on illegal drugs originally got hooked on legal opioids, prescribed by a physician after an accident or surgery. Other times, a hereditary predisposition is a major factor. And still other times, sensitive souls who simply cannot handle life find substance abuse an irresistible means of escaping their tough reality. In any case, people with such addictions are *people.* That is what I sought to portray in the story, **"The Revival."**

While I met homeless people who had at one time been professionals, the character of the Peacemaker is not based on any one of them. He is a composite of many of those who, while educated and at one point successful financially, have found their lives on a serious downward trend.

Upon reading the above words, some might say, "Then these stories are not *true.*" But truth is independent of whether a writing is fiction or nonfiction. Some reportedly nonfiction writings have very little truth in them. Hitler's *Mein Kampf* was nonfiction, but I would certainly contend that it is not "true." The truth of these stories derives from their picturing some truths about the human condition. All of us are in some sense "fallen angels"—persons who have fallen from our full potential as human beings. But being alive means having hope, hope that we can do better, that we can rise higher. These stories are ultimately about that hope, and I would attest that hope is true.

1. "Data and Trends," United States Interagency Council on Homelessness, January 1st, 2025.

Body Double

(This story first appeared in Stevan Nikolic, editor, Adelaide Magazine, Volume 1, 2015)

"I get the feeling you don't believe me," I said as I grabbed a stick and stirred the dying fire. I looked past its struggling flames to the bearded man wearing a Lakers jersey and a painter's cap.

"What makes you think that?" he said, looking around the circle at the others. "Hey, I mean, don't we all believe her story? She says she was the body double for Judy Garland—what's not to believe?"

"Actually, I meant 'stand-in,'" I said. "I was a body double for her a couple of times, but mostly I was her 'stand-in.'"

"Right, stand-in." He rolled his eyes, looked at Crazy Jane and shook his head. "God knows, she's old enough." Then he looked back at me. "So, when can we expect the invasion of flying monkeys?"

"Well, that certainly shows you weren't listening," I said. I straightened up and glared at his shifty eyes. "Everyone knows Caren Marsh Doll was her stand-in for *The Wizard of Oz*! I was her stand-in for her later roles: *The Pirate, Summer Stock, Easter Parade*, and *A Star is Born.*"

The man fell back onto the ground and started laughing hysterically while beating his hand against one of the pillars holding up the bridge. "Right! Right!" he said when his laughter abated enough to get out the words. "And now you're slummin' with all of your other famous friends livin' under the frickin' Burnside Bridge!"

"I believe her." The words had quietly left the mouth of an older man who sat partially hidden in the shadow cast by the pillar. I had seen him before. He was always grizzly, but the beard never seemed long. His face appeared perpetually sad, but kind.

"Really?" the Lakers guy said incredulously.

"I believe her, too," said Crazy Jane. "I went to Julliard and I'm here with you. I was good, too. Not playing for any of you street trash, but I was good. Played the viola until I broke the strings—"

"God, that was a frickin' movie! *The Soloist.* And it was a Black dude. If you're goin' to lie—"

Crazy Jane hugged herself tightly and rocked violently back and forth. "Not lying! Not lying! Not lying!"

"Apologize." The directive came from the man in the shadows. He voiced the word respectfully, but with the authority of one used to being listened to.

"Hell, I should apologize for tellin' the truth to a crazy bag lady?"

"Come on, Cole, you know you should."

"Whatever. Sorry," the guy I now knew as Cole said. "Hell, you're not any crazier than the rest of us. You say you went to Julliard, I guess you went to Julliard."

Crazy Jane stopped rocking.

"And I shot Osama bin Laden." This claim came from a young Black man with broken glasses, wearing an Army fatigue shirt, as well as the baggy pants so popular with the young. "Shot him right between the eyes, and now all of them radical Muslims are out to get me. The gova'ment won't protect me, neither—I know too much about what's really goin' on, an' they would just as soon have me dead, too. Got all of the CIA out lookin' for me. Every building in Portland is bugged. That's why I'm out here on the street."

Cole shook his head. "Really, Snake?"

"Hey, mark my words, one day you're goin' to find me dead out in the street somewhere, and you'll know it was the CIA."

"I believe you about the buildings," said Crazy Jane. "I stay out of most buildings. Sometimes, though, I think they are watching me when I do my business in the street."

"Sick bastards." said the man who called himself the Snake.

"Well, all of you have inspired me to tell my story," said Cole. He stood up. "You see, my real name isn't Cole. It's BILLY FUCKIN' IDOL! Woo-hoo!" Then he pretended that he was playing a vertically-oriented air guitar, which he stroked like a giant erection coming out between his legs. “It’s a nice day for a white wed-ding—”

“Okay, I’m out of here,” I said, standing up. Admittedly, the move would have been more dramatic at a younger age, but at ninety I no longer got up quickly from sitting on a city street. “I am a lady of sophistication, and I do not have to tolerate such language and vulgarity.”

“Oh, give me a break!” said Cole.

“Come on, stay,” said the man in the shadows. “Hey, we’re all out in the street. We have to tolerate stuff from each other. That’s just Cole’s way.”

“Hell, yes,” said Cole, sitting down again as he spoke. “Don’t be such a priss. Besides, that’s the way he really talks. I listened to a concert the old dude played at Riverfront Park. Every time he talked about himself, he said, ‘Billy Fuckin’ Idol.’”

“Stop saying that or I will leave!” I know a ninety-year-old woman waving a fist is not really intimidating, but I did it anyway, just to drive my point home. “Portland is a big enough city that there are other places to go.”

“Stay,” said the Snake.

“Stay, stay, stay—” said Crazy Jane as she started rocking back and forth once again.

“Tell us about Judy Garland and being her body double,” said the man in the shadows.

I eased myself back on the ground.

"I should tell you I really loved Judy Garland," I said. "She had elegance, even though she hardly saw it in herself. She saw herself as a rather plain girl in a world of glamour. Like I said, I was not usually her 'body double.' That term is only used if you take the actress's place to dance or do something dangerous. Or today, to do a nude scene, but they didn't do that sort of thing then. People had class."

I gave a caustic glance in Cole's direction, but he ignored it.

"Anyway, Judy could really dance, so I rarely danced for her. Although I could have. I was quite a dancer in those days. Danced with Fred Astaire once, for *Easter Parade,* although it didn't make it past the cutting floor. And I did dance for Judy a time or two in a couple of her other movies—*Summer Stock, A Star is Born*. She was having her troubles. Well, she was depressed a lot. Mostly, though, I served as a stand-in. I took her place when they were setting the lights for a scene. I was good for that, because I was her height, weight, and approximate skin color."

"Ever do it with Gene Kelly?" Crazy Jane asked.

"What? You mean, dance?"

"I sure would have done it with Gene Kelly. Now *that's* being a body double!"

I ignored her. "Stood in for Judy Garland a few times as a mother, too. I couldn't count the number of times I held Liza Minnelli on my lap. Such a cute little child."

"I would have done it with Liza Minnelli," said Cole.

My jaw stiffened, and I reconsidered whether to say any more.

"So, what happened?"

I glanced toward the man in the shadows. While I still could not see much of his face, his question came to me gently and with tender sympathy.

"Well, they paid stand-ins okay, but they didn't give us much of anything in the way of health insurance. So, of course, my husband got cancer. He had been working as a grip, and didn't have insurance either. I had a little saved up, but it was quickly gone. Couldn't work much because I had to look after him. By the time he died, there was no more money."

Colored lights flashed from behind me. I turned to see the source.

"Talkin' about getting thrown out, here we go." Cole stood up even as he spoke. The Snake got up and ran. Crazy Jane grabbed her shopping cart full of belongings and followed him.

"My friends and I aren't harming anyone, officer," I said. "We're just sharing stories."

"Doesn't matter, sweetheart," the officer said while strolling up beside us. "You can't be doing it here. Sorry, but it's the law. And you can't be lighting fires like this either."

No sooner had he said this than his partner came out of the car with a fire extinguisher and sprayed it on our fire. Smoke, soot, and chemical fumes billowed up into my eyes and I started choking.

The first officer walked over close to me. “Are you okay? Pardon me, but aren’t you a little old to be out on the street? Why don’t you let me take you to a shelter?”

He put his hand on my shoulder, and I jerked away.

“I’m okay,” I said. “But no shelters. I don’t trust shelters. I’ll go. You don’t need to take me anywhere. I’ll go. Okay?”

“That’s fine, that’s fine,” said the officer. “I’m not going to hurt you. I haven’t seen you on the street before, though. Are you new around here?”

I looked into his eyes. They appeared sincere.

“Yes, well, I am new to these streets. I lived for a while in an apartment over on Yamhill, until they threw me out. Before that I was down in Los Angeles.”

“LA, huh? I was raised there. What’s your name, sweetheart?”

What did he want with my name?

“You must be new on these streets also, officer.” The words came from the man who had been in the shadows, but who now strolled up beside me. He was about six feet tall, a foot taller than I am, and he had salt and pepper stubble on his face. Still, his clothes seemed clean and well-kept. He was the only one of the others who had remained. “Because if you had been here long you would know that sharing one’s real name is a lot to ask from someone living on the street.”

The officer nodded. “And you, if you won’t give your name either, at least how do you identify yourself?”

“They call me the Peacemaker.”

“‘The Peacemaker,’ huh? Well, I’m a peacekeeper, so we’re kind of related in our work, and I’ve got to ask you to warn your friend here that these streets are a dangerous place for an old woman at night, okay?”

“I’ll do that.”

“I’ve been taking care of myself for forty-two years, ever since my husband died,” I said, without even so much as raising my voice. “I can take care of myself now, too.”

“She used to be a body double for Judy Garland,” the Peacemaker said.

“Well, I mostly was just her stand-in.”

“Really?”

He didn’t believe me.

“Well, I don’t know a lot about Judy Garland, other than she supposedly took her own life,” said the officer. “But I’m glad you have decided not to follow in her footsteps in that regard, and I trust you won’t expose yourself to needless dangers on our streets.”

“I’m not crazy!” I said.

“I’m sure you’re not. And now my partner and I have to get back to our rounds,” he said. “So, you two need to move along. Please don’t let us find you starting any more fires on the street.”

“You won’t, officer,” said the Peacemaker.

The officer joined his partner in the squad car, which then pulled away.

"You don't have to take care of me!" I said to the Peacemaker. "I am neither a child, nor a senile old woman!"

The Peacemaker shrugged. "Have you met my friend, MAX?"

I started picking up my things, which consisted of a purse and a backpack, both filled with my most essential items. "No, I have not had the pleasure. But whoever he is, Max does not need to take care of me either."

"MAX is the Metropolitan Area Xpress—the light rail."

"Oh, of course. I've heard of that. But I've been doing everything downtown. I don't need to go anywhere else, so—"

"Getting out of downtown is not the point," he said with a gentle smile. "You can travel on MAX and sleep in the seats all night, and no one will bother you. So, if you would allow me to buy you an all-day pass—"

"Oh . . . that would be nice, I guess. But you do not have to pay my way. I have a little."

"I insist," the Peacemaker said. "I have seen *Summer Stock* and enjoyed it immensely. You can consider it a token of my appreciation for your role in making that movie happen."

It was a gentlemanly thing to do. I accepted.

We found seats facing each other, so both of us could stretch out. It helped, of course, that hardly anyone else rode the train at that hour. I put my backpack next to me and looked out the window. I had forgotten the joy of going somewhere, even though I knew we would be covering the same parts of the Portland metropolitan area over and over that night. I could see the hundreds of cars passing by on the highway, each one going somewhere important, and I knew they could look out their windows and see the train, and they could believe we were all going somewhere important as well. I liked thinking that.

I looked at the Peacemaker. "You know, you were the first person since I came to Portland who believed my story. Thank you."

He smiled at me and gave me a little nod.

"I think because you believed my story, the others around the campfire believed it too, at least a little."

"I think they did," he said. "I think they really did."

I glanced out the window again. "I mean, that's not to say that even you might have doubted it a little."

"Everyone on the street has fallen from something a little higher," he said. "That's what I think. So, I believe people's stories, until they tell me differently."

"Even Crazy Jane's? I mean, I have to admit I had a little trouble with that one myself. And the Snake—you didn't believe him, did you?"

The Peacemaker smiled. "Well, believing is what I do. But it is true that I do not always do it perfectly."

"As I suspected."

His smile broadened even more. "I tell you what, I do believe the spirit of his story. I believe he served our country, did some killing that made him fearful of retribution, and does not trust the government to do right by him."

"That describes every veteran on the streets. And Crazy Jane?"

He shrugged. "Have you ever eaten over at the Baptist church's free kitchen?"

I nodded.

"Next time you eat there, duck into that ornate reception hall they have by their sanctuary and listen. After you do that, we can talk again."

The Peacemaker pulled off his coat, put it on the chair arm for a pillow, and curled up as best as he could on the short bench seat. I followed suit, but even as short as I am, I had to squeeze into the seat. As I started to settle in, a question eased its way into my mind. I nudged the Peacemaker with my foot, and his eyes opened.

"So, what did you fall from?"

He looked at me for a moment. "What?"

"You said that everyone on the street has fallen from something a little higher. What did you fall from?"

He closed his eyes again. "That conversation is for another day."

******

Standing in a food line is not one of my favorite experiences. The people driving by are looking at you, judging you. They wonder why you cannot make it on your own, and when they ask themselves why, they figure that it's drugs or alcohol. I haven't had a drop of alcohol since my wedding in 1940, and the only drug I have ever taken was the one the doctor gave me when my husband died in 1969. It didn't take away the pain.

The other thing about standing in line is that it feels so much more competitive than I want to feel. You are hungry, and every person ahead of you is an obstacle rather than a person. I fight that feeling, but it's still there.

Inside the church, the aromas coming from the hot food so overwhelmed my senses that I almost forgot the other reason I came. Checking out what that ornate reception hall might reveal didn't seem like a very pressing matter while I relished seeing servers heap meatloaf, green peas, and real mashed potatoes onto my plate. I didn't rush through the experience of eating this food, since each bite not only filled the emptiness in my stomach, but also a certain emptiness in my memory—my memory of when food brought primarily comfort rather than just sustenance and served as a gathering mechanism for bringing together family and friends. I hungered for those times. Still, for some reason, I had been having trouble lately remembering many of them specifically. Now, however, homemade mashed potatoes and green peas brought back a picture of my mother's face. Meatloaf, my husband's favorite, resurrected his once-again healthy presence beside me.

Only when the last white fluff of mashed potatoes was gone from my plate did I hear it. A soft, muffled melody coming from somewhere within the church.

I walked through a set of doors, and past a desk where a young woman sat. She motioned for me to stop.

"The music! I just want to—"

She waved me on with the smile of an aficionado.

At the top of the stairs the music pulled me down a hallway into what I knew must be the reception hall the Peacemaker had spoken about. Rich walnut paneling flanked stained-glass renderings of biblical figures, and elegantly framed portraits of what I assumed were former pastors. Overhead arched a domed ceiling featuring sky lights and more stained glass. In the center of it all stood a mahogany grand piano, and on the bench of that piano sat Crazy Jane.

She played what I recognized as Chopin's *Nocturne in B-flat minor #9*, and she played flawlessly.

I marveled at how the person at the piano bench seemed like someone else entirely from the frightened, disoriented person whom I had sat beside on the street. Her fingers flowed across the keyboard, and her body swayed with power as the music seemingly infused her battered soul.

I walked up closer, not wanting to disturb or embarrass her at the prospect of an audience, and yet something within me couldn't keep quiet.

"I didn't believe you," I whispered, but within her range of hearing.

She looked back and smiled. She did not respond verbally, but her music transitioned effortlessly into the more recent classic which she knew would delight me, "Somewhere Over the Rainbow." No, I had never danced it in performance, nor was I a stand-in during the movie from which it had come, but ever since I had met Judy Garland, it had spoken to my imagination. Now, once again the piece spoke to my heart. In my mind's eye I could see that rainbow which had been missing from my life; and perhaps my mind played tricks on me, but I could also envision my younger self in a gingham dress, dancing along a yellow brick road.

I lost myself in a dream.

"Was it all a dream?" I asked when Crazy Jane finished playing. She cocked her head like a confused puppy. "When I was a child, my mother always used to say I had an imagination like no child she had ever known," I said. "And of late my imagination is all I have had. I don't know. You know what they say about old people. I have these memories, but were they ever any more real than a yellow brick road or flying monkeys?"

Crazy Jane turned to her piano keys and played them once again. This time the melody which came spoke to my whole body.

"Get Happy" from *Summer Stock.* It was one of my clearest memories, dancing to that song, but what amazed and delighted me was not how my mind remembered it, but how my body did as well.

Sing Hallelujah! Come on, get happy! The words danced through my mind as my ninety-year-old feet began to tap, and my arthritic body began to sway and twirl as if I were once again in my late twenties. I shuffled under a church dome to music about a judgment day and strutted past stained glass with words singing in my mind about taking the Lord's hand. My body became the song, and my mind just watched. Still, the watching was pure pleasure, as if after a whole lifetime I returned to my adolescence, rediscovering orgasm. My heart raced, but in an excited, not a frightened way; and all the time I had a picture in my mind of Gene Kelly in the wings, watching me.

The music so took hold of my spirit that I only slowly realized Crazy Jane had stopped playing. The clapping in the wings alerted me.

From the hallway I had come down earlier emerged a man with salt and pepper stubble, applauding with enthusiasm. "Bravo! Bravo!" said the Peacemaker.

I looked at Crazy Jane, who rocked back and forth on the piano bench.

"I missed that note," she said. "I missed it. I'm no good. No good. I missed it. I never should have tried that song. Never should have tried. Never should have tried."

"What note?" I asked. "You were great!"

"She won't hear you," said the Peacemaker. "Right now, the only voices she can hear are in her mind."

"But she played so well! Can't she see that?"

"No. Seeing it would be scary for her."

"Why?"

The Peacemaker shrugged.

"You told me to come here, and I found that maybe she was telling the truth. But why did she say she played a viola?"

"Perhaps she did. I know she played the flute and the violin. Anyway, she can't carry a piano around on the street. And she had seen *The Soloist.* I managed to score a couple of tickets, and I gave one to her."

"I danced!" I said, my mind not letting me flee too far from the moment.

"I saw!"

"I didn't even know I could do that anymore."

The Peacemaker laughed. "Well, your body apparently did."

I smiled as the memory refreshed itself. Then I looked again at the Peacemaker. "You said we would talk later about what you had fallen from."

He put his hands in his pockets and looked down at the floor, but before he did, I saw escape in his eyes.

"Of course, maybe this still isn't the right time," I whispered.

He stood there for a moment, shaking his head. Then he looked at me and smiled himself. “I fell from what was perhaps the greatest height of all.”

“You are an angel, fallen from heaven?”

He shook his head. “I was a teacher.”

******

It rained all that night, but the next morning the sun broke through, and that meant I awoke to the sound of birds singing, and a rainbow lifted over Portland. All that day I sat and imagined yellow brick roads for people on the streets of my city. Perhaps I was a body double after all.

I never did find the Peacemaker again. Three nights after he had seen me dance, the police officer who had ordered us to disperse from under the bridge, found him at the base of that same bridge, dead.

I never learned how he had fallen from being a teacher, or what kind of teacher he had been. I didn’t need to know. Mostly, I just wished I could have let him know he really hadn’t fallen so far.

Thunder Rolling Down the Mountain

(This story first appeared in T.D. Johnston, editor, Short Story America, Volume V)

The thing about having only one leg is that it's much easier to mount a horse. You might not think so, but six inches of stump doesn't take a hell of a lot of clearance to swing it over a saddle. At least that's what I've always found.

So, there I sat astride my favorite steed, a golden Palomino. She stood steady, gazing out at the horizon with me, waiting for just the right nudge from me to send her galloping in whatever direction I would choose. There was no need to choose quickly. We could saunter off to the north, where the great river *Wimahl* runs; we could trek to the west and the ocean white men call Pacific, or we could head directly east to the mountain the Salish people called *Wy'east,* named after the brave warrior who fought *Klickitat* for the heart of the beautiful maiden *Loowit.*

Of course, I have always been called by the spirit of the mountain myself. To ascend a mountain is to be drawn by the Great Spirit to his own *tipi*, to be granted the freedom to see all that a god sees, and to understand how the land that is my home connects to all that is beyond it.

I was getting ready to head east, when a voice surprised me from down below.

"Where do you think you're goin', Chief?" A white man's police officer. He had other officers with him, while I was accompanied only by a *squaw*. I would have to be careful.

"To the east, to the mountain you call Mount Hood. I go in peace and mean you no harm."

"Really? What's your name, Chief?"

"Roy."

"Gotta last name, Roy?"

"Just Roy."

"Well look, Roy—that horse ain't takin' ya to Mount Hood, or any other place outside of this park, for that matter."

White men never understand the power of a Nez Perce on his favorite horse. I smiled.

"This is a golden Palomino, a Quarter Horse bred for speed. Should I call upon her to do so, she could turn and be gone out of your sight before you could even remember where you left your car."

The officer shook his head. "Yeah, I don't think so, Roy. First of all, that isn't a Palomino; it's a gilded statue of a European war horse. And second, if you look over your shoulder, the *squaw* sculpted to ride that horse is Joan of Arc, the world's most famous female warrior, and she's lookin' a little pissed right now that you've hijacked her horse."

Little did he know that Nez Perce *squaws* always look pissed. I wondered if I should expose his ignorance and make him lose face with his other officers.

"You see, Roy," he said, speaking a little arrogantly for someone probably twenty-five feet below me, "that's a famous statue of a famous lady. Teenage girl who led an army to free the French people from an oppressive invader. The statue is dedicated to those who lost their lives in World War I."

"Against an oppressive invader?" I said, mostly to myself. *Perhaps she could be more helpful than I had previously known.*

"Roy, I'm sorry," the officer continued, interrupting my thoughts, "but you've got to get down from there. And, if you don't mind my asking, how in the hell did you ever get up there in the first place?"

I noticed that the earth-bound are always searching for the secrets of those called into the sky. Still, he seemed to have a good soul. I lifted the rope near the noose-end of the lariat I had used to snare this steed. "My people are raised around horses, officer."

"So, you lassoed the head of Joan's horse, and you—what?—pulled yourself up by your arm strength alone?"

I nodded. "In a wheelchair, all you've got is your arms."

"Nice," he said. "Still, you've got to get down from the statue, Roy. You're distracting the drivers passing by."

So again, the call to surrender to the white man. I scanned the horizon. I scarcely could view the trees without my eyes being pulled away toward the droppings of white culture—including the traffic he had spoken about. Even the steed on which I rode was made as a tribute to a white woman who had never even seen this land and given in honor of a white man's war fought on the other side of the world.

"Tell me, officer," I said, "had Joan of Arc fought with the French alongside my people against the English invaders of this land, would they have given her a statue?"

I could see in the officer's eyes that my question had gotten past his ears to his soul. His eyes softened. His jaw lost the rigidity of one standing for the law. No quick answer came.

Four birds left their branches in the nearby trees and found new places to rest their spirits before the officer raised his eyes toward me and spoke again. "It's not always fair, is it, Chief?—life, that is. Sometimes you're just screwed, and it makes no difference what you do."

I nodded.

"Would it help for me to mention that they have a statue of Chief Joseph downtown near Portland State?"

"I know," I said quietly, "but they gave him no horse."

"True," he said, walking up a little closer. "Probably afraid he would be like you and ride it off through the streets of Portland."

"Yeah, he would."

The officer took hold of the handles of my wheelchair and turned it around toward me. He looked up at me again.

"Still, I got to tell you once more to get down from there, Roy," he said. "I know it ain't fair, but it's my job, and I like my job."

I looked back at the birds in the trees. It seemed they had stopped singing in order to see how our little drama would play out. I bet they knew, just like I knew.

I lifted my hands to the heavens. "Hear me, my chiefs! I am tired; my heart is sick and sad. From where the sun now stands, I will fight no more forever." I swung my stump over the saddle and dismounted. Yeah, super dramatic. Über–Nez Perce. It would have probably been more so had I not forgotten to grab my rope—and that I was still over twenty feet off the ground.

******

I have to admit, when you live your life on the street, it's kind of nice spending a little time in the hospital. Warm blankets.

But it's also true that when you live your life on the street, they don't let you stay very long, and so as I wheeled my way from the front entrance of Providence Medical Center, my head still throbbed, and my formerly good leg felt sore and unsteady whenever I put weight on it. They say that if I hadn't grabbed for Joan of Arc's leg on the way down, I probably would have broken that other leg. Even as it was, the impact caused sprains and threw me off balance, so I hit my head on the concrete base of the statue. Thus, my throbbing head.

When I reached the sidewalk, I noticed the police car parked on Glisan. I had seen the officer who climbed out of the driver's side door before.

"Don't tell me, officer. Now I've taken Joan of Arc's wheelchair. I'll give it back. I would hate for her to head into battle without it."

"Glad to see you're feeling better, Roy. By the way, I'm Officer Warner."

He held out his right hand, and I took it. "Wonderful. You have a last name, and I have a first name. Together we could be a whole person."

"Okay, then," he said, "I'm Officer Karl Warner."

I smiled and let go of his hand. "Still just Roy."

"Where are you heading this morning, Roy?"

I shrugged. "Not back to the statue, if that's what you're worried about."

He sat down on a nearby bench. "You know, Roy, if you would drop the cynicism just a little bit, I might be able to be your friend. I want to make sure you're going to be okay."

I looked into his eyes. He had a good soul. "I'll be okay."

"But you have to stop drinkin' and climbin' up on statues."

"Friends don't let friends drink and climb."

He laughed. "That's right."

"Except I wasn't drunk," I said. "If you really want to be my friend, you need to know my spirit. I do not surrender my spirit to drink."

He cocked his head to one side and looked at me with narrowed eyes. "I gotta say, Roy, you seemed a little out of touch up there on the statue."

"I don't drink." I spoke quietly, so he could hear the power of the truth. "I'm hooked on something even more dangerous."

"And that would be—"

"I still dream," I said. "You should try it. It's hallucinogenic."

"So I've heard. Just don't let your dreams lure you into high places, or else next time your dreamer self could be splattered all over the concrete."

A honk came from Officer Warner's police car, where his partner looked flustered.

"I gotta go," said the police officer. "Where are you headin'?"

"Downtown. Pioneer Square I guess."

"Is that where you hang out?"

"Most of the time. It's what we Indians do—lurk around pioneers and look dangerous."

"Need a ride?"

I thought of some guys I knew who might give me a hard time if they saw me getting out of a police car downtown. "Maybe you can give me a ride over to the MAX line."

"Sure."

I wheeled over to the car. He opened the rear door, and I maneuvered into the seat. Officer Warner folded up my chair and tossed it into the trunk. As I fastened the seatbelt, I noticed Warner's partner didn't look too pleased.

"We haulin' in the Injun," he said as Karl Warner slipped into the driver's seat, "or are we just starting a friendly taxi service?"

"Don't get all bent out of shape, Wilson," Karl said. "It's good community relations. We're taking him over to the MAX line."

"You got money for the MAX line, Tonto?"

My eyes did not feel comfortable looking at the man called Wilson, so I looked out at the traffic as I responded to his words. "If I were Tonto, I would have a horse."

Wilson turned around and glared at me. "Then how about if I just call you Sitting Bullshit?"

I let him wait a little while for his answer.

"Did ya hear me, Sitting Bullshit? Or are ya deaf as well as dumb?"

"He's not our prisoner, Wilson, so stop trying to brow-beat him." Officer Warner looked at me in the rearview mirror and smiled. “Besides I happen to know that Roy here is Nez Perce, while Sitting Bull was Lakota Sioux and Tonto was Potawatomi—unless, of course, you’re talkin’ about Jay Silverheels, who was a Mohawk from Canada.”

Wilson now turned his glare toward his partner. “God, you’re a walkin’ Injun encyclopedia, aren’t ya? Of course, I wasn’t talkin’ to you, I was talkin’ to your soulmate, Sitting Bullshit back there.”

It appeared that Officer Warner was about ready to lose his temper, so I intervened. “Actually, I kind of like ‘Sitting Bullshit.’ It suits my spirit. Nothing is more healing to the spirit than a little fittingly applied bullshit. So, I accept. And, yes, I have money for the MAX line.”

“Well, hallelujah, now I can sleep at night.” Wilson diverted his attention to the neighborhoods we were passing.

“You know, Roy,” Karl Warner continued, “I’ll tell you a secret. The reason I know so much about various tribes is that when I was a teenager, I always wished I was an Indian. Studied all about ‘em.”

“Really?” Having wished throughout my teen years for the opposite, this was intriguing.

“Not surprising to me,” said Wilson, still looking out his window. “Anything but a regular American. Me, when I was a teen, I wanted to get laid. That’s what’s called ‘normal,’ Warner.”

"Yeah, I was anything but normal in my teen years," said Warner as he turned the car into the little parking lot by the MAX station. "I always felt like an outsider. Probably still applies. I identified; Indian making his way alone through the wilderness, fighting all the battles more civilized people were afraid to fight. And, yeah, Wilson, you cow turd, I wanted to get laid too, but I thought the girls would think my Indian self was hot."

The car stopped and I opened the door. "Let me know how that works for you, Officer Warner. Because it sure as hell didn't work well for me."

Karl Warner got out of the car and went back to the trunk, where he pulled out my wheelchair, unfolded it, and put it, brake set, in front of me.

"I'm not sure you're going to be able to do this, Roy," he said, "but ya gotta keep your battles off public property now. It will only get you arrested, and there goes your freedom."

"Public property, huh?"

"Yes."

I looked into his eyes. I never tired of looking into kind eyes, even though there was much these eyes did not yet see. "Isn't that property which belongs to us all?"

I love it when I ask questions people can't answer.

******

Coming back downtown was like a crash landing. Instead of soaring into the air from horseback, I was suddenly having to look up at everything: the tall buildings rising overhead, the lights which told me to "walk" or "don't walk" (as if I could), and even the people standing in line for a free meal at the Baptist Church.

At least they knew me at the church. They called me Roy, and they smiled.

After receiving my food plate, I pulled my wheelchair in next to a man I had seen many times, a man who called himself the Peacemaker. One of the church volunteers carried my plate and sat it in front of me. The shame of it all quickly jolted my spirit. I was Nez Perce, a tribe which, along with the Salish, were the most ancient residents of this land. Yet I depended on whites not only to provide my food, but even to carry it to my table.

"Enjoy your meal, Roy," the volunteer said. I didn't know her name, but I thanked her.

"Hey, Roy," said the Peacemaker. "I haven't seen you around much. What have you been doing with yourself?"

The Peacemaker had a salt and pepper beard which seemed just a few hours older than a five o'clock shadow. It was well trimmed. I had always wanted to be able to grow a nice beard, but that was not a gift the Great Spirit had given to the Nez Perce. I always thought it would be a nice way to hide scars and moles, among the other imperfections on my face.

I took a bite of the chicken casserole. "Nez Perce are naturally nomadic. I have been reminding myself that the world is bigger than Pioneer Square."

The Peacemaker nodded.

"So, why do you call yourself 'the Peacemaker'?" I asked before savoring another bite of the casserole. "Among my people, a man must earn such a name."

I'm not sure why I asked the question. On the street you learn that a person's name is given as an expression of trust. It is one thing that you can own and control; in a world where there is so little, where that applies. I glanced over at the man in between bites, and he seemed deep in thought as to whether he was going to grant me this gift. He was halfway through his meal when he looked in my direction.

"I believe sometimes a name is not what you have earned from your past, but something you want to shape your future. Do you think your people might agree?"

I grunted. Again, I'm not sure why. I remember as a child an old man who grunted at stories told around the campfire. With him it seemed profound.

"You see, Roy," he continued, "there is so much conflict in the world. In my past I was a big part of that conflict. I wanted what I wanted, and the needs of others didn't matter. It destroyed my life. I had a wife once. A son. A home. I kept fighting battles which were all of my own choosing, and I lost. Now, no more."

I glanced across the table and noticed two other men who had frozen in place, their loaded forks in front of them, their eyes vacant.

"On the street I've noticed that about everyone is fighting a battle, and most of them are losing. I figure they all need a Peacemaker. Someone to help them put a halt to all of the conflict inside of them. I mean, look where we are." He motioned toward the walls of the church dining area. "'Blessed are the peacemakers, for they shall see God.'" Then he added, "Jesus also said, 'Blessed are the meek, for they shall inherit the earth.' Maybe that is what would bring you peace, you know."

"When my people made peace with the white man," I said, speaking quietly but not meekly, "they lost the earth; they didn't inherit it."

The Peacemaker looked into my eyes. "Maybe the one you need to make peace with is not the white man."

He would not release my eyes for what seemed like hours but was probably only several seconds. When he finally did, I quickly finished my meal.

"How did you lose your leg, Roy?" The question came from a man across the table. Maybe he thought he was changing the subject.

"In battle," I said. Then I wheeled my chair around and left the table.

******

It is amazing how fast you can go in a wheelchair when you are fleeing the truth. Eight blocks separate the church from Pioneer Square, and I had traveled that distance before another thought even entered my head.

When people asked about my leg, I normally did not tell the truth. *Why had I done so this time?* “In battle” normally was a lie. I had an elaborate story of how I had fought in the first Gulf War, helping to continue the tradition of the Code Talkers, Native Americans who fought in World War II. I was helping to decipher codes, and generals depended on my knowledge and insight. We were attacked, and a grenade exploded nearby when I was carrying a buddy to safety. I saved him but lost my leg.

That wasn’t really the battle. Maybe Warner’s partner was right. Chief Sitting Bullshit was a good name for me.

I had told the truth when I told Officer Warner I do not surrender my spirit to drink. Of course, I didn’t say I never had. There was a time when drinking alcohol was my only refuge in the battle with myself. When you drink enough, all the stuff you don’t want to think about is purged from your mind. For me there came a night when I had drunk an adequate amount of this spiritual anesthetic, and I found myself on the west side of the city where the MAX train travels faster between stops. All I could see was that I had left my jacket on the other side of the rails, and I thought I was fast enough to beat the approaching train.

When I awoke in the hospital, they told me I was lucky I survived at all. I wasn't so sure. Still, I went into rehab and now I don't drink.

When you are Nez Perce—scouting your way, living off a paltry disability check and wheeling your way through downtown Portland—and you have given up drink, you are an unarmed warrior.

So, it was as an unarmed warrior I now surveyed the urban valley ahead of me. The mountains surrounding this valley were skyscrapers made by human hands, and the valley itself was a two-block square sunken plaza of brick, concrete, and tile called Pioneer Square. Store clerks and corporate executives gathered there for lunch alongside the homeless, students on break, and shoppers escaping from the nearby shopping mall. It was a nice summer day, and so there was a band playing below, and people were relaxing and reading on the steps.

I wondered what they all would think if a screaming Indian would suddenly descend upon them, thumping down the steps in his wheeled, aluminum horse? *Yeah, they would probably just call the cops. Probably Officer Warren again, and I would be embarrassed.*

My battle really wasn't with these people anyway. I remembered something Officer Warren had said, and I turned my wheelchair back toward Eleventh Avenue. I boarded the free trolley to Portland State University, disembarked, and wheeled my way over to Jackson Street.

There it was: a bronze statue of Chief Joseph. I slowly wheeled my way up right in front of the commemorative piece. Already I could feel in my spirit this was the place I needed to be. I had seen it before, but I had shied away from it. Why? Perhaps it had been shame. Shame to come before such a father of my people and show him what I had become.

It was indeed true that the statue portrayed the great chief without a horse, but this did not take away from his dignity and power. The statue was bronze and was about ten feet high. He had a blanket draped over his left arm and a walking stick in his right, but his eyes were what drew my attention. The eyes were attentive and wise, the eyes of a man who let nothing pass before him unexamined, the eyes of a man who took charge of his world.

The eyes shifted and looked at me. I know, that does not make sense when you are looking at a statue, but it was true, nonetheless. They looked at me and penetrated my spirit.

Why do you come before me, my son?

The lips had not moved, but I had most certainly heard the voice.

"I don't know who I am or where I belong, Oh father of my people." His eyes were on me. I could feel his sorrow. "So much has changed since you walked this land."

Yes, we were contented to let things remain as the Great Spirit Chief made them. They were not and would change the rivers and mountains if they did not suit them.

"What should I do?"

Reclaim the land.

"I have no weapons! And they are mostly good people."

He was patient with my confusion. *The earth is the mother of all people, and all people should have equal rights upon it. I did not say "wage war."*

I felt ashamed that I had misunderstood, and I hung my head. "The man Jesus said, 'Blessed are the meek, for they shall inherit the earth.' But I do not understand how that can be."

This Jesus speaks the truth. When I was a child, I learned from the Christian missionaries. They said some things I left as dust by the roadside of my journey. But they also taught some good things.

"But then you lost the land where your father was buried. So did it really help that you were meek and a peacemaker?"

"Blessed are the meek, for they shall inherit the earth. Blessed are the peacemakers for they shall see God." I feel those truths in my spirit.

"But unless I go back to our little reservation, all I have is this wheelchair, and occasionally a place under a bridge."

I did not challenge you to inherit the bridges—or tall concrete buildings, or houses where one can hide from the Great Spirit.

"Inherit the earth?"

Inherit the earth. Reclaim it. Yes.

"But I am not a wise and powerful leader. I am just Roy, a man with one leg who speaks to statues."

Then you need a new name. I grant you mine.

"Chief Joseph?"

No, not my Christian name. My Nez Perce name, Hinmaton-Yalaktit. Thunder-rolling-down-the-mountain.

"I could never be worthy of such a name!"

As I looked, the face of the statue was no longer looking at me, and his spirit no longer spoke. His eyes once again focused on his own horizon, a horizon which I could not see.

I whirled around in my chair. I did not know where I was going; I simply knew I must go.

Inherit the earth.

The words echoed over and over in my mind. They echoed as I raced past the buildings which housed the classrooms of Portland State University. They echoed as I sped through intersections, ignoring lights and dodging cars. They echoed as I rolled past the taller buildings of downtown Portland to the MAX station at Pioneer Square. When the Blue line came heading east, I got on it right away. I gave it no thought.

Inherit the earth.

The words now whispered in my head, timed to the clickety-clacking of the train on the rails as it picked up speed.

Inherit the earth. Inherit the earth. Inherit the earth.

We sped past asphalt-laden interstate highway, mini-malls, houses, apartments, and townhouses, all of which began to look the same after a while, but very little earth.

When the train came to the end of the line in Gresham, I got off and sped down the sidewalk, as if my wheelchair knew where I was going, even if I didn't. I reached Highway 26 heading east and turned in that direction. I wondered what people thought as I wheeled past, head down, determined to go somewhere, no longer sitting in a concrete and tile square, waiting for nothing.

My arms were burning from the strain. I wondered how long I could go on. As the vision came to my mind of where I was going, I wondered even more. It would take days.

I was now out beyond the residential and commercial fringe of the city and rolled down a hill past tall Sitka Spruce, trees which lifted my eyes to the heavens. I smelled their sweetness and relished the wind rushing past, caressing me; the same wind which made the tree branches flutter and sway. Deer grazing by the road ran off into the forest, perhaps to tell their friends of the return of the Nez Perce to this land.

As I came to the bottom of a hill, I saw the Sandy River to my right. The embankment leading down to it was not too steep, so I pulled my chair to the side of the road, braked it, then scrambled and slid my way down to the river itself.

The water was chilly! I took off all of my clothes except my undershorts and crawled my way in until the water swept up over my back. I shivered with delight. The life of the river washed over me and infused my soul with its energy. I looked up and saw an eagle flying high above me, a sign which my people have always seen as a messenger from the Great Spirit, a sign that brought honor and courage.

I cupped my hands, drew from the water, brought it up to my lips, and drank deeply. Then I did it again. I know, I was supposed to think of the dangers of *giardia*, but at that moment I was no longer a twenty-first-century man, withdrawing from the dangers of an untreated world; but rather I was immersing myself in the life of the earth. While I had not even considered the need to bring food and water on my venture, what I thirsted for was not just water, but *that* water—water fresh from the mountains; water supplied by the earth, my mother.

When I pulled myself out of the water, I became aware of my hunger. That hunger drew me to a bush of salmonberries, and I ate my fill.

After I had dressed and crawled my way back up the embankment, I should have been exhausted, but I was the opposite. I felt like I had been reborn.

That evening, before the sun went down and I stopped to sleep on the pine needles of the forest, I got my first view of what I now knew was my destination. Capped with snow, even in the summer, and majestically rising over the surrounding hills, stood the mountain I would claim as *Wy'east,* and not Mount Hood. I still wasn't sure of how I would do it. To ascend such a mountain in a wheelchair would not be easy, straining with all my might for each foot of ascent gained. But the eagle would fly high above me to give me courage, and the Creator God who made the mountain, and spoke from within the mountain, would draw me with his power. I would go to the top and see God. I would look down from near the summit and see the distant valleys where my people and the Salish people once roamed, and once finished, I would roll down as if on the wings of the eagle, and I would shout out to the wind,

"Thunder once again rolls down the mountain!"

Getting Lost

Once when I was walking past the Union Gospel Mission a scruffy old man asked me if I was lost. *God, I hope so!* That was what came to my mind, but I didn't say it. I didn't say it because I don't talk to scruffy old men—or men at all, for that matter. I don't talk to them, and I don't look them in the eye. So, I just shook my head, and quickly went on, making a note to myself not to go past the mission again.

You see, getting lost is not as easy as some might think. I've been working at it for nearly a year now, and there are times when I think I've succeeded. Nobody in Portland knows my real name, and many don't even know I'm a girl. I feel pretty proud of that. I watched *Boys Don't Cry* four times before I left home, studying how Teena did it. I watched the way she walked and dressed and carried herself. There were other scenes that were too hard to watch. I just fast-forwarded through those.

Of course, she was a *lez.*

I'm not a *lez.* I just don't trust men. So, a few days ago I noticed one was following me. They do it all the time, ever since I took to the streets of Portland. They do it because I'm pretty, I guess. Sometimes I think of ways to become un-pretty. One girl I know just became fat. She ate everything she could get her hands on. I don't think I could do that, though. First of all, I'm not sure I could get my hands on that much food anymore, and the churches around here only let you have seconds if everyone else has been fed. Besides, I don't like how I feel when I'm fat. One time before I left home, I developed a little bit of a paunch, and it scared me. I couldn't eat anything for two days.

Anyway, the guy who was following me scared me because he had that look in his eye. Yeah, the one my father used to have when Mom wasn't around. But I don't want to think about that.

To be fair, sometimes I meet women who have that look in their eyes, too. Like there was this older *skank* down at the YWCA who watched me taking a shower. She told me I looked like a young Phoebe Cates, whoever that was. I guess they filmed her naked taking a shower in some movie. Anyway, I finished my shower really fast and put my guy clothes back on. Like I said, I'm not a lesbian.

The guy had followed me for a while and so I started running toward the library. I knew my street family hung out there. No guy was going to try to jump my bones with my street family around me.

So, the reason I know I'm not a lesbian is 'cause when I think of Art Alexakis, I get all hot. You know, the lead singer from Everclear. I wouldn't mind him watching me in the shower. Yeah, sick, I know—he's as old as my dad, but I used to listen to his music all the time when I lived at home. Whenever I felt like I needed a good cry, I would listen to "Father of Mine." He knew what it was like to have a father who wasn't a father, and he's a really good father himself. A friend and I saw him playing with his little daughter in a park once. But the song that would get me all hot was "I will Buy You a New Life."

I turned the corner and was starting to run up the stairs to the library when a hand grabbed my shoulder from behind. It was the guy who had been following me. I screamed.

He looked around nervously. "I . . . uh . . . I just . . ."

"I ran from you!" I shouted. "I showed you my 'Don't try to talk to me' face! So why are you trying to talk to me? What do you want from me?"

"I'm sorry. I saw you dancing around Pioneer Square and I thought you looked cute. I—"

"Well, stop! Stop talking to me!"

I turned and ran up the steps into the library.

I should know better than to dance, but it's one of the few pleasures I allow myself. When music is playing somewhere, my body starts to dance. The way I move, I know people can tell I'm a girl. Sometimes I even feel I have to toss off my ball cap and my overcoat to be able to move freely, and then people really know that I'm a girl. I've got to stop doing that.

The library is the place where my street family gathers when it's cold. Except we have to be careful, because we like talking to each other, but the librarian keeps wanting to "shush" us. I saw them all sitting at a reading table. I went over to a magazine rack, grabbed the current issue of *People,* then pulled up an empty chair beside them.

James, an old Black dude with a gray, scraggly beard, leaned over and whispered to Maria. "Hey! Isn't that one of the Kardashians who just sat her little white ass down across from us? Kim, ya' think? Or maybe Kourtney?"

James is my street dad, and maybe the only man I trust, probably because he's gay. Maria, an illegal immigrant from Mexico, is my mom. She used to take care of kids in a real home before the government tried to get her deported.

"*¡No, es imposible!*" Maria said, also in a whisper, "*no es una* Kardashian as street tough as dees girl. *Es verdad,* Princess Leia?"

Maria had used the street name of the one I called my little sister, who sat to my right. She is fifteen, while I am sixteen. We call her Princess Leia because she always seems to be off on another planet.

"I saw some TV actors once," she said, "they were filming by the courthouse. Does anyone hear a bird? I thought I heard a bird. They probably don't let birds in the library. Hey! You know what? I found a dollar coin near the MAX line track this morning. I should get a candy bar—"

"Damn, Princess Leia!" injected my Black sister, Camille, "How many people ya' got in that little noggin o'yours, huh girl? You jes' keep up that conversation with ya'self, 'n the rest of us, we goin' to talk some more about our little Miss America Emily here, okay?"

Princess Leia didn't seem offended at all. She smiled at us, and then her eyes drifted off toward the ceiling. Nobody wanted to ask what she saw up there.

Camille looked at me. "So, *what up,* Emi-Lou?"

Okay, my name is Emily, not "Emi-Lou," but Camille likes to call me that. Actually, my family is the only one around here who even knows my name is Emily, so just keep that part to yourself, okay?

"I had to get in here off the street because some guy was hassling me again. Real pain in the ass."

"What?" said James, raising his eyebrows. "Some guy trying to put his hands where they don't belong? I swear, I may be an old queen, but—" He was getting up from the table.

"No, Dad. Nothing like that."

"What, then?" he said again. "Tryin' to pull you down some dark alley? Talkin' to you as if you were some cheap little tramp?"

"No, not exactly."

"What then?"

I had been trying to focus on my magazine, but I could see the effort was useless, so I shut it. "This guy, you know . . . *looked* at me. Then he followed me all the way from Pioneer Square, and he told me, well, that he thought I was cute when I dance."

"*Ay, Carumba!*" said Marie. "Such a devil should not be allowed to live!"

James sat down and started laughing, which was the last straw for the librarian, who came over and told us if we did not quiet down, we would all have to leave.

After she went back to her desk, James looked at me and shook his head. "Oh Emily, Emily!" he whispered. "Was the guy at all good-looking?"

I sought to recollect the face. "Yeah, I guess. Blue eyes, strong jaw. About six inches taller than me. Nice smile."

James cocked his head in a questioning manner. "And what exactly about that offends you?"

I shrugged.

"You could've at least put in a good word 'bout me to him, ya know."

Maria slapped him on the shoulder. "Right! He chasing dees beautiful young girl because what he really want ees old Black gay guy. What you think, *hombre*?"

Maria looked across the table at me, took my hand and patted it. "Emily, *mi hija,* are you sure you are not—how you say?—dee lesbian?"

"No!" I said, catching myself before raising my response to a shout, "I am not '*dee lesbian.*'"

"You are sure? 'Cuz you know we still love you anyway, *verdad?*"

"I'm not a lesbian!"

"She wants Artie the Old Fartie," said Camille, shielding her words with the back of her hand, as if it were a secret even from me.

"Who?"

"Artie the Old Fartie—Art Alexakis, the lead singer for Everclear. She has the hots for him. He's like a zillion years old."

I bristled. "More like fifty."

"Too old for this chick," said Camille, "and I'm five years older 'n you!"

"Emily, sweetheart," said James, flicking his wrist at me, "far be it from me to get into yo' bizzness, but didn't ya leave home cuz the old dad was jumpin' ya bones?"

I nodded.

"So, now that yo 'free at last! free at last!' are yo loins really achin' that much for someone who is ya dad's same age?"

Princess Leia stood up quickly, swept her hand palm down across the table and shouted, "Safe!"

The reference librarian had us heading out the front door in less than thirty seconds.

******

Normally when the Space Princess says something we smile and roll our eyes. But my street family took her library pronouncement as something rather profound. We were sitting on the cold steps in Pioneer Square, huddled together, watching some break dancers down below.

"I gotta hand it to you, Princess Leia," said Papa James, "you just may have hit on something there, back in the library."

"No way!" I said. "Who knows where her head was?"

"Nope. Sorry, Miss America, but she nailed you with that one. It's pretty safe lettin' yo'self get all hot over someone ya ain't never goin' to have. While lettin' yo'self get interested in someone standin' right before ya, someone who might hurt ya, someone who might stomp yo little heart into a bloody pulp, that's scary as hell."

I didn't say anything.

"I had a boyfriend once," said Princess Leia. "He kissed my knee when I skinned it falling off the jungle gym. I don't play on jungle gyms anymore, but I can climb trees. I like the trees they planted around the square. I wonder if anyone tries to climb them? I wonder if librarians have ever climbed trees? Maybe I should get a book on trees when they let us back in the library!"

"Hell yes, Princess," said Camille. "You go, girl!" She turned to me. "Me, I don't think there is a scarier creature on God's green earth than a good-lookin' dude. 'Cuz the good-lookin' on the outside is just cover for all the poison in his weaselly little brain. So,

I changed my mind. I think you were smart stayin' away from that dude."

James had turned reflective. "My longest affair was with Tom Cruise. It lasted from the time Jerry left me in 2002 to the time Mister Mission Impossible dumped on Brooke Shields on TV cuz of her postpartum blues in 2005. Probably wouldn't have lasted quite as long had I ever really met him. So, you're right, Camille. Us good-lookin' dudes, we all just poison inside."

"*Mira, Chiquita,*" said Maria, "we not the ones you should talk to 'bout dees. Me, I never choose well da men. Last one, he beat me. Before that, he do da drugs. But that don't mean you no find *tu amor verdadero.* You are so . . . so beautiful . . . *muy hermosa.*"

That's when I discovered the tears streaming down my cheeks.

"Oh no, girl," said Camille. She put her arm around me. "You don't need to go there with the tears 'n all. Hell, Maria there's right. You flat out gorgeous, girl! Course I gotta admit I'm as jealous as hell. Every dude I get even a little interested in, I gotta make sure he don't see you without that hobo coat 'n dime store ball cap, cuz if he do, hell, all I can do is put a bowl under his mouth to catch the drool, cuz he ain't lookin' at me no more."

The tears were now dripping off the end of my chin, and I was sniffling every few seconds to keep my nose from unloading its goo into my mouth. Maria gently wiped my face with some tissue.

"Beauty hurts," I said.

The thought had been forming in my head for weeks, hell, maybe for most of my life, but it had never found expression in those two simple words. “It does. It hurts.”

“What do you mean, Emi-Lou?”

“It just does. It makes you a fuckin’ target—you’re a target for every guy in the world who thinks that your being pretty is some kind of come-on to them to paw at you and put their filthy hands on your crotch, and . . . and . . . tear off your pajamas when you’re in bed, and you just want to be safe and sleep in your safe bed, but you can’t because your mother is gone, and he wants to stick his hairy thing in you, stabbing over and over like he’s trying to kill something, and you keep telling him to stop, but he won’t, even though you’re crying, and when you’re crying he’s supposed to hold you and comfort you—isn’t he? Isn’t he supposed to comfort you when you’re crying?”

I became aware that I was flailing at everyone around me, although my eyes were so blurred by tears that I could hardly tell who anyone was. Even so, I knew who the arms belonged to that grabbed hold of me and held me so tightly I knew I could never break away. I knew the smell of the cheap perfume. I knew the voice that at first only expressed her own wailing but then started to form words. Princess Leia, though no bigger than myself, rocked me like a child, and as she rocked, she now gave voice to the message we both needed to hear:

“Safe! Safe! Safe!”

******

For three days my street family would not leave me alone. Wouldn't leave Princess Leia alone either, for that matter. We hadn't known about her father.

When they were finally convinced I was not on the verge of slitting my wrists, they let me go my way. I needed that. I knew they cared, but I needed to get away from their constant watching, like I was some fragile glass vase getting ready to fall off the shelf.

It was raining hard that day in Portland. It almost always rains, but the rain is normally a gentle one that tickles your face and arms, like pebbles thrown by a friend at your window. This rain was a street flooder, driven by the harassing wind, not at all a friend, pushing against you like it doesn't want you there. Normally in such a rain I would go into the library or hide under a canopy, but today I had to walk. I had to walk, not to get somewhere in particular, but to pump blood to my brain and focus my mind.

I found myself down by the Congregational Church and noticed the sanctuary door was unlocked, with a sign encouraging people to come in and pray. I don't normally go in churches—well, except to eat, I guess. My mother used to take me to church as a child, and as I reached my adolescence, it was a chance to escape my father. Even there the men, including the ministers, were looking at me with those eyes; and I knew it was not a place where I could hide and feel safe. But this would be an empty, or near empty, sanctuary. I pulled the door open and went inside.

My clothes were sopping wet, and I didn't want to drip water all over the floor and pews, so I took off my coat and ball cap, and hung them up on the coat rack. The moisture had made it through to my shirt and jeans, but at least they were not dripping, and the sanctuary was warm.

Again, I was hoping for an empty sanctuary, but as I walked down one of the center aisles, I became aware that that was not the case here. A man sat toward the front on the outside aisle; I recognized him as the man who they call the Peacemaker, a homeless older man, perhaps in his late 40s or early 50s. I could tell, however, that he had not noticed my entrance, and he was fully absorbed in the moment. I sat down quietly and looked around.

The pews of the church wrapped around the front stage, where there was a pulpit carved out of dark oak. The organ pipes fanned out across the front wall, and appeared as a series of large pencil boxes, prepared to write a story in music. Large stained glass windows were to either side, featuring characters from biblical times. While beautiful, I did not recognize any of these characters in my own life, and so I focused on a simple wooden cross rising above it all.

The cross was something I could feel.

After gazing at this cross for some time, I noticed the man had moved to the center of the sanctuary and had fallen to his knees, raising his hands toward the cross and weeping.

I considered for a moment whether I had ever seen a man cry. I hadn't—well, except on television, and that doesn't count because there, they are always trying to make what is strange and unreal seem real. Here a man was crying, and for all I could see, it was because of a deep spiritual pain, a pain like mine that was tearing him apart. His eyes were gazing at an empty cross. His tears seeded my own.

Now the Peacemaker had prostrated himself fully on the floor, with his hands stretched out in front of him toward the cross. I looked up at that ancient emblem myself, and for a moment an image flashed in my mind of my own form upon that cross, and the pain on my face was the pain I had seen a thousand times in the mirror of my parents' home, the blood being the crimson flow from where the crease of my hips met the middle of my naked thighs. And then in a moment the form changed, and the blood of my thighs trickled down off the soft-tufted beard of an ancient man's chin. And I cried as I had never cried before.

I don't know how long I had been looking up at that cross, but I know what drew my eyes away. Down the aisle next to me, walking with his head down, preoccupied, was the Peacemaker. When he reached the pew three rows in front of me, he noticed me and stopped. For a moment I could see the look in his eyes, the look

I had seen in men's eyes so many times before. For some reason it didn't frighten me as much this time, but it did cause me to be reminded that my shirt was wet and form-fitting, and I wore no bra. I crossed my arms in front of my chest, but all the while I kept my eyes fixed on his. It was the transformation in those eyes which I found fascinating. For a moment he looked away, closing his eyelids and scrunching them up. But when he opened them again and looked back at me, they transitioned from sadness to compassion to shame and back to sadness again, all within seconds.

"I hope it was okay that I was watching you up there," I said. "It helped me a lot."

"I didn't think anyone was here," he said quietly.

"Your pain—I felt it. That is what helped."

He shook his head slowly and closed his eyes again. "I'm glad it helped you. But you should not look to one such as me for help." When he opened his eyes again, they were looking away, toward the exit. "The pastor here is a woman. Talk to her. That is all I can say."

He ran to the door and left me there alone.

******

One thing about the rain in Portland is that when the sun does come out in a cloudless sky it is renewing to the soul. All that is green appears freshly created, and people linger on every corner, exploring the wonder.

That is the kind of day it was the morning after my encounter with the Peacemaker. I walked all the way up to Washington Park, and surveyed the beauty down below that hill, the beauty of Portland when it is effused with sunlight. It was a five-mountain day, a day when you can see all five volcanic peaks on the city's horizon. Still, even a beautiful day couldn't keep me away from Pioneer Square for long. My street family always reconnected there. It was a place where you could meet a total stranger and make up stories about her or him in your mind. It was the place where sometimes you could see the movers and shakers of the city sitting on benches or steps like normal people. It was where you could feel the pulse of life.

It was for reflection that I came on this day. I hadn't gone to talk to the woman pastor the Peacemaker had recommended to me. Maybe I just wasn't ready yet, or maybe I already knew at some level what I needed to do to find my peace.

When I reached Pioneer Square, I noticed straight ahead of me a section of stairs where no one was sitting, and I started to walk in that direction when something drew my attention to a bench about twenty yards to my left. There, sitting by himself, was the dude who had followed me to the library steps. He leaned forward with his elbows on his knees, looking down at the sidewalk, not allowing himself to be distracted by the persons passing on every side. An old boom box on the seat beside him sat silent.

He was kind of cute. Tall with blonde hair, a strong jaw, and blue eyes. He reminded me of a young Brad Pitt, except that Brad Pitt always seemed confident and in control, while this guy showed nothing of the sort.

I felt a strong urge to look for other choices, and indeed as I looked to my right, I saw my street family kicking a hacky sack around on the sidewalk. I like playing hacky sack. So, when I sat down on the bench next to the "Oh, I just love your cute dancing" dude it was as much of a surprise to me as it would have been to them, had they been looking my way.

"Okay, here's the deal," I said as he looked into my eyes, "we can hang out sometimes when I'm not with my street family, and you can play songs on that antique box of yours, and maybe if I feel like it, I'll dance a little—"

"Yeah, that's—"

"I'm not done! Did you hear a pause? I'll dance a little and if you want you can dance too, but if you watch me, I don't want you watching my ass, okay?—Answer with your head, not your words—okay?"

He nodded.

"And sometimes we can talk, too, but I don't want you thinking you can talk me into anything I don't want to do, and NO TOUCHING! Well, no touching yet, anyway, because I'm still figuring some stuff out, okay?"

He nodded again.

"You can talk now."

"Oh!" he said. "Uh . . . that's all okay, I guess. I'm Kyle. You gotta name?"

He was pushing it, and I let him know with my eyes.

"I mean, you dance great and all, and I like the idea of hangin' with each other, but I need to know what to call you, don't I?"

I said nothing.

"I gotta admit, I was feeling pretty bummed, not only because . . . well, you weren't exactly nice to me in our first encounter—"

I looked down at my hangnail and picked at it.

"Yeah, and, this whole city has been crapping on me ever since—nothing like Hays, Kansas, where I was raised—but now I get this great opportunity to hang with Hot Dancing Girl, and I don't want to call her just Hot Dancing Girl, so—"

"Emily."

"Your name is Emily?"

"No. I just have this weird disease where I blurt out the name 'Emily' every now and then. What do you think?"

He looked down at the sidewalk in front of him again. "It's a pretty name. I like it."

"Yeah, it would still be my name even if you didn't like it." I don't know why I was being such an asshole. *Don't judge me!*

I shifted my gaze back toward my street family. They had stopped playing hacky sack and were all looking my way. I smilingly flipped them the bird and returned my attention to Kyle.

"So, what brought you all across the country from Kansas?"

"As good of a place as any to get lost," he said. "When I'd had enough of my dad beating the crap out of me, I spun around in a circle, picked a direction, and headed as far away as I could. Turned out to be Portland."

I looked into his eyes for any trace of the scariness I had earlier fled. All I saw was a younger version of the Peacemaker.

I pointed to his boom box. "Got any CDs for that antique from Everclear?"

"Yeah."

"Got any songs of theirs you think I might want to dance to?"

He smiled, leaned over, and pulled out a CD case from under the bench. He thumbed through his collection, and quickly found the one he was looking for, which he surreptitiously placed in the CD player. He pushed the number without having to look at the song list. Then he smiled at me again and motioned toward our brick dance floor.

The smile grew across my face before I even heard the first strumming of the acoustic guitar. Somehow, I could tell he knew what the right song was, and I was dancing and twirling when it came:

"Bum, bum, bum, bum-bum-bum-bum (ooo-oou).

Bum, bum, bum, bum-bum-bum-bum. (Yeah!)"

My body gyrated, and slithered, and my head was bangin' as the first words came ringing across the square; and as Art Alexakis reached the chorus, Kyle stood and joined me in the dance:

"I will buy you a garden where your flowers can bloom . . ."

And indeed, the blooming we shared lifted our hearts to heaven as our feet danced in celebration. Then when the song reached the crucial words, the words which had pulled me alive from the wreckage of my early adolescence, the words which time and again had been the light shining in the pit where my father had thrown me screaming, I could no longer just dance. Rather, I stood with my arms reaching toward heaven and my joy penetrating the sky, while my lips mouthed the words.

"I will buy you a new life,

Yes, I will!"

I'm not sure how long it was from the time the song ended, and the time it stopped echoing in my heart. All I know is that when I finally looked at Kyle, I looked into eyes filled with my tears streaming down the young man's cheeks. And I know one more thing. At that moment he could not help himself, and he reached out and touched my hand.

I didn't even scream.

In a Foreign Land

I begin my story to say I steel don' speak well dee Anglish . . . dee language of dees country. *¿Comprende?* So, I talk to Emily, *mi hija*—well, she not really, but she treat me like *tu madre,* so I call her *mi hija*—and she say she halp me. Okay? So, Emily, you go now.

Yeah, trust me, I'm Emily and it's good that I am telling you Maria's story, because I live with her on the streets of Portland, Oregon, and even I don't always understand her English sometimes. Of course, I'm only sixteen, and never finished school, so there's that.

Anyway, let me start by saying Maria wasn't even sure at first that she wanted to tell her story. She is one of those "illegal immigrants" you hear some people complaining about sometimes. Personally, I think this land belongs to God, and how can a human being God created be illegal in his land, tell me that? Still, ICE doesn't see it that way, so she's got to lay low, you know what I mean? Me, I know all about it because I'm hiding from other shit, but I don't want to talk about that.

Maria is from Guadalajara down in Mexico, a place I really didn't know hardly anything about until I met her. Not a great place, at least not for the people who live there. Between the cocaine cartels and corruption in the government, a lot of people live in fear, and there is much poverty. She and her husband Carlos crossed the border illegally to make a better life for themselves, but things were tougher here than they had expected. Carlos got discouraged and started to drink a lot, and when he drank, he beat her. But, you see, here's the thing. When you're here illegally, you can't get police protection or file for divorce—

"Emily, psst! Psst!"

Okay, just a minute. Maria is trying to talk to me. *"What is it, Maria?"*

"Digo que . . . tell them I no want divorce. Tell them I good Catolico. Tell them!"

Yeah, she wants me to tell you that she really didn't want a divorce because she is a good Catholic. That's true. She's always going to Mass. But I think the truth is that she wanted to get away from him and couldn't find a good way to do it. Anyway, she left him and came here to Portland. But now, of course, she has to look over her shoulder all the time, not only because she's worried about ICE or the border patrol catching her and deporting her, but because she's worried about Carlos coming and beating the crap out of her.

"Es verdad."

So, that's why at first, she didn't want to tell her story. I mean, you can understand that, can't you? But then she decided it was important for people to know her story, so they would know what it is like for someone like her on the street.

"Emily! Psst! Psst!"

"What, Maria? Do you want me to tell them your story or not?"

"Tell them, I lie. Tell them my name no es 'Maria.' Tell them I am Carlotta. Carlotta from Tijuana. Tell them. And . . . oh! . . . tell them I no live een Portland. Tell them I live een Seattle. Tell them."

"Uh . . . it's a little late for that, Maria. They know this is Portland. Just let me tell the story, and we'll figure out later . . . you know, what to do. Okay?"

"Okay."

So we'll pick up her story from the time she came to Portland.

******

Maria came to Portland scared and alone. And yet she was reassured by the thought that being "scared and alone" was a hell of lot better than being frightened beyond measure by the one sharing your bed.

Right away she found a Catholic church with a Mass in Spanish. She couldn't say it felt like home because home was such a scary place, but the church had always been a refuge for her, and with that refuge in place, she could face anything.

Some people at the church helped her to learn more English, and they also helped her fill out some applications for jobs. At first, getting a job was not a problem for Maria. You could tell that she was a hard worker by looking at the calluses on her hands and by seeing the steely-eyed look of determination on her face. And, of course, people knew you could pay a Latina immigrant a lot less.

Maria got a job as a nanny, cleaning a big house up in the West Hills, and taking care of an eight-year-old boy and a five-year-old girl.

"Fue el paraíso . . ."

Yeah, well, Maria has taught me a little Spanish, and she just said that it was like heaven to her. She ate what they ate, and that was always the best. She had her own apartment in the house, and even that apartment was bigger than any place she had ever lived. And she had one more thing I know was especially important to her. She had a family. She had not been able to have any kids with her husband. Given how that relationship turned out, I suppose that was for the best, but it left an empty place in her heart.

The family's two children became her children. For over a year she spent more time with them than the parents did. She fed them, made sure they got off to school in the morning, and welcomed them home from school in the afternoon, always preparing for them a welcome home snack. She couldn't help them with their homework, but she was a hard-nosed disciplinarian and made sure they had it finished before they watched any television or played video games. She loved them and held them when they were sad.

They loved her. Yeah, maybe too much. I think the parents got a little bit jealous.

She doesn't know—and I don't either—whether it was the jealousy or maybe some political pressure from immigration or some of the family's Republican friends, but they fired her. No reason given.

"*Mi corazón aplastado*."

"Okay, Marie, I don't really know that one. I think I heard it on a Santana CD, but still—"

"My heart . . . eet break."

Yeah, it hurts.

So, Maria was back on the street. Only this time things were harder. The immigration crackdown had made it harder to get a job. Maria felt like she was being watched all the time. ICE was even showing up at her church. She stopped going for a while, but that was hard on her, so after a while she went back. Maria needs her church more than anything.

She was thinking of moving to a different city and getting a new start when she met us. Her street family, that is—me, my Black sister Camille, and my little sister we call the Space Princess because she's a little crazy. I didn't tell anyone at that time my name was Emily, because I was hiding myself. I was pretending I was a boy; I wore boy's clothes and called myself Sammy. But this story is about Maria.

I remember the day. Maria sat across from us for the meal they serve the homeless at the Baptist church. She looked hungry and scared. I could tell she was trying to eat slowly so it would last.

"They will let you have seconds once everyone is served," I said. I had used my deepest voice, the one I had practiced so many times.

"*Muchas gracias, muchacha.*"

She said "*muchacha.*" I didn't realize at the time that the Spanish word indicated she realized I was a girl. Had my little disguise worked she would have said "*muchacho*." Maybe it was because she had recognized a kindred spirit. And maybe that recognition was also why, when we had all finished having seconds, I said what I said to her.

"You wanna hang with me and my street sisters?"

Her eyes opened wide, and she blinked a couple of times. That's when I realized she probably didn't understand teen street lingo. Hell, for all I knew they still hung people down in Mexico. So, there was more than one language difference separating us.

"I didn't really mean 'hang'. I meant . . . do you want to have someone to be with for a while?"

She smiled and nodded.

It wasn't until Maria joined us that I realized how all of us on the street are just trying to make it in a land where nobody else thinks we belong. Maria's story is kinda my story, too.

We slept that night, as we normally do, underneath the Burnside Bridge. James, who is now my street dad, always slept nearby to protect us. He is gay, so we felt safe from him, but he is also a big Black dude, so he did offer protection from nighttime assault.

Maria was unsettled that whole first night together. She jumped at every noise, and when you sleep on the street there are always noises. I didn't sleep well that night either because of her. I guess I was hearing with her ears. After that night we decided to sleep in a different place each night. No need to be too predictable.

The next day I was surprised that James wanted to hang with us during the day. He seemed to have a special concern for Maria's well-being. He asked a lot of questions about her life, how she got to this country, and what situations she saw as dangerous for illegals. Because he knew a little Spanish and she knew a little English, they figured things out together. It all took me by surprise, because of him being gay and all. I mean I was used to men being nice to women because they wanted to get into their pants. I knew I loved my street sisters, but the thought that a man could love someone when it had nothing to do with sex was entirely new to me. I thought about that one for weeks. Eventually it struck me that maybe he loved me and my street sisters too, and that was why he had been protecting us at night. Go figure.

"*Y yo te amo también.*"

"Maria, if you're going to interrupt, use your English words!"

"Okay. I . . . uh . . . I love you, too. And I love *mi amigo Chames . . . mi familia preciosa.*"

"Okay, Maria, you've got to stop crying now. Maria? Maria, you're going to get me crying, too, so stop! Oh, my God, give us a minute."

******

That's better. So, back to Maria's story. I don't know if ICE was really so hot on deporting her, or if it just seemed that way to us. When I first left home six months ago, I thought I saw my father on every street corner, coming to claim what he thought was his own. Not that he really gave a damn for me, ya know. Anyway, maybe it was the same with ICE and Maria.

There was a day, though, when our fears became real, and we almost lost her. We had heard rumors that ICE was going to do a sweep of downtown Portland, but there had been rumors before, and nothing had happened. There was a salsa band playing in Pioneer Square, and like all bands they get to play there, it was free. Maria wanted to go because it reminded her of home, and the rest of us like any kind of music that is free. Yeah, salsa band, rumors of an ICE sweep—we should have known. It's easy to see that now, but at the time we were tired of being scared and not doing anything that was any fun.

So, Pioneer Square has steps descending on all sides to a center courtyard where the bands play. People can sit on the steps, or you can go all the way to the bottom and dance around in the center courtyard, ya know? Maria was smart. She wanted to sit at the top of the steps where we could look around and see danger coming. Me, I wanted to dance. So did the others. We still feel a little guilty about that one. So, we all went down to the center court and started dancing, and she didn't want to be alone, so she joined us.

I have some great moves when it comes to dancing, and James?—well, he's gay, so enough said. Camille dances like a stripper high on crack, so I generally act like I don't know her when it comes to dancing. The Space Princess, on the other hand, reminds me of some Disney character, prancing through a field of flowers and songbirds—which isn't so strange when you think of it, because that's probably where she thinks she is. We just leave her to her world.

Maria didn't dance at first, but it wasn't long before the music of her country completely grabbed hold of her. It started with a little sway of the hips and then evolved into a shimmer and shake throughout her whole body. But the part I especially liked was when the dancing reached her facial expression, coming out in a sexy sassiness in her eyes and her pursed lips. I had no trouble seeing the dancing partner she imagined to be with her, and I wondered who she was remembering dancing with, and even whether they had ever performed together. I liked seeing her so happy and free.

I'm not sure how long it was before the ICE agents appeared, patrolling all sides of the square, at the top of the stairs. By the time I spotted them I was sure it was too late. Yes, there were a lot of Spanish speaking people in the crowd, but they seemed to be checking every one of them, and sneaking Maria out between them would be a major challenge. While trying not to appear too panicky, I let the others know what I saw and told them not to look. Actually, I'm pretty sure Maria couldn't have looked, because she froze in place the moment I told her. I don't always think quickly, but I did this time, and I called the family into a huddle where we all swayed to the music. Okay, Maria was maybe teetering a little more than she was swaying, but still from the outside and up at the top of the stairs, I think it looked like just a different kind of group dance. The agents would not have been able to see our wide eyes and open mouths.

"What do we do? What do we do?" Turns out my quick thinking had its limitations.

Everyone was looking back and forth at each other with mouths hanging open, and because I couldn't stand that, I lifted my head and looked up in the direction of Yamhill. People say there are no coincidences, but that God directs each moment. I really don't know about that, but what I do know is at that moment I saw the man who calls himself the Peacemaker looking right in my direction. I could tell right away he understood our dilemma, and he gave me an okay sign. Then he immediately walked to the nearest ICE agent and took hold of his arm. The man looked his way, and I could see recognition flash across the agent's face, even from that distance. He flashed a huge smile and gave the Peacemaker a hearty handshake. Then the Peacemaker put his arm around the man and gently guided him toward the corner of Sixth and Yamhill, making that whole side of the square virtually unguarded. I couldn't believe my eyes! It was like a huge door had swung open. I knew it wouldn't be open long.

"Okay, everybody, keep it casual here," I said, "but the Peacemaker just got a guard to move over, and we have an opening, so let's move!"

I skipped up the stairs like a person without a care in the world, and the rest of my street family followed suit. We were halfway down Fifth Avenue past Taylor before anyone even spoke.

"Damn, what the hell just happened?" said Camille.

"Moses happened, that's what!" said James. "That dude is a Moses, yeah, he is. Parting the Red Sea, so God could let his people go! Praise God and hallelujah!" And James did a little dance.

Maria, however, collapsed to her knees and crossed herself.

"What I don't get is how he did it, and why he did it," I said. "How did he get that agent to move?"

******

We never did learn for sure how the Peacemaker had provided for our escape, but we all had our theories. The Space Princess was convinced it was a Jedi mind trick—*This is not the immigrant you are looking for!* Either that or we had been sprinkled with fairy dust that made us invisible. I figured if there was such a thing as fairy dust, the drug companies would have made it too expensive to use on poor street people, so I eliminated that one from my own consideration.

Camille said she had heard the Peacemaker used to be a professor at Portland State, until he had gotten involved in some scandal and made to resign. Anyway, ever since he had been a kind of Robin Hood protector of the poor. She figured maybe the ICE agent on that side was a former student he had distracted or maybe even convinced to let us pass. That was a damn good theory, I would say.

Still, Maria and I mostly go with James' original thought: God had sent us a Moses. In this foreign land, God had sent one caring man to divide the waves of political oppression for one crucial moment, so we could walk through unscathed.

"Gracias al Señor!"

Yeah, Maria still keeps doing that, thanking the Lord and crossing herself. I'm not sure how she can keep doing it when we are still homeless and ICE is out there looking for people like her, but maybe it's just one of those things you hold onto.

Sometimes you just gotta believe.

The Top of the World

(This story first appeared in Stevan Nikolic, editor, Adelaide Magazine, Volume 2, 2015)

I'm standing on the top of the world
Though others less schooled might say
The top of the steps
Of the Multnomah County Library, Portland, Oregon,
Downtown Branch.

The top of the world
Neither bitter nor cold,
The warm air of my insulated soul rises above it all
Rises above the shivers of uncovered hearts on windy street
Rises above the teeth chatter of icy word
Rises above the distance
Those below see as safe.

The secret of my warmth
Emanates from the friends within

The hallowed walls of this repository
Friends not of flesh, but of word
Friends who speak with the gentleness of
Ink and paper
I will myself to know them all
I will myself to carefully peruse
Each book
In this bastion of learning
Each book
In this library where I live.

This poem launches my morning. Each word the same each day. One change of tense, one alternate word, one variance of cadence, and I wouldn't know which door to enter, which place to sit, which book to read. I would have to go back and start my day all over again. The words begin their flow toward my mind, starting with my first breath of morning air, drawn in from my sleeping place underneath the Burnside Bridge. By the time I finish my ascent to the top of the library steps, they are flowing onto my tongue, and I whisper them to my soul, to let my tender inner core know I have arrived at home. You notice I did not say, "I have arrived *from* home," because the library *is* my home. I have a right to claim it as my home because I am there more than anyone else in this city; more than the people who work there, because they have shifts; more than the people who use it, but have jobs elsewhere they must attend to; more than the so-called patrons and county officials who made the decision to close it on certain days, closing ME out, but are hardly ever there themselves.

This library is my life. *Do I not have a right to life?*

People judge me. They do. They think that because I wear secondhand clothes which often do not fit or match (I *know* they don't match—do you think I am blind?), that I am unschooled and ignorant.

Do *they* comprehend Stephen Hawking's argument for a Universe closed in on itself, which he makes in *A Brief History of Time?*

Do *they* understand what Paul Farmer says about how our country's policies have contributed to the problems in Haiti and other underdeveloped countries?

Have *they* wrestled with grace and legalism in Victor Hugo's *Les Misérables?*

Do *they* know what Dostoevsky's novels meant to people in Russia seeking faith under communism?

They think they know what is happening in Iran and the Middle East. But do they even know who Mohammed Mossadegh was? Do they know that Iran used to be Persia, and that Cyrus the Persian was the one who freed the people of Israel from bondage and sent them back to rebuild their home country? Do they even remember what happened in Iran-Contra?

But they call *me* ignorant. They say,

"Mister Yeats, he speaks of his life in a poem
With words that don't even
Rhyme."

Thus saith the masses addicted to the poetry of Hallmark.

As I look out at those masses from the top of the library steps I just want to scream; I want to scream, "Stop running! Learn the TRUTH!" But I know they would never pay attention. They might throw a dollar or two in my direction, thinking that is what I want (and what *else* do these bums want, anyway?), but they would never be so generous with giving their minds, with giving their ears, with giving what I want above all else.

So, I turned from my search and ran for shelter.

"Hey, Mister Yeats!" said the young man who unlocked the doors. "How are you doing today?"

"An answer to the status of the moment
Lies not in that instantly evaporating breath of time,
But in the million moments before, caustically churning out
The billion fearfully chaotic moments after,
And in the time one takes
Humbly off-balance, but alert,
To envision them all."

The young man paused and looked into my eyes. "Okay. Well, I'll have to think on that a while, won't I?" And he moved on.

Why do I even bother? They all want plain speaking, when all I can offer is a flow of feeling which comes from beyond me.

The Peacemaker came up behind me, the *second* person from the street to enter. He reached to put his hand on my shoulder but paused short of that goal as he saw me already flinching.

"Not wishing to intrude, Mister Yeats," he said, "but I liked your entry poem today. I would have given it an 'A.' Do you ever write them down?"

Why was he asking that? To judge me? I shook my head.

"Well, I am a fan," he said, "a fan of poetry, and of yours in particular. Just wanted you to know." He moved on.

At least the Peacemaker listens to me in his small, inadequate way. I know many of the people in the library, and none of them want to listen to me at all. I'm not sure why. Afraid, perhaps.

I quickly found my place in my reading; not in one particular book, but in the stacks of books. I was working my way through section 215, "Science and Religion," and was now ready for my next selection, Frances Collins' *The Language of God.* All about DNA, arguments for Creation, and how faith and science relate. The book would give a contrasting perspective to Stephen Hawking, so I was looking forward to it.

I wasn't five pages into the book when a street family sat down next to me. I don't mean an actual family thrown out on the street, but rather a variety of homeless people who had decided to be a family to each other while in their transient state. I had encountered a number of such families, but I had spurned that direction myself. Didn't need it. My books were my father, mother, sister and brother.

Anyway, I had encountered this street family before, and they all talked like magpies, even in a library designed as a sanctuary against such garrulous interference. I tolerated it for about five minutes before putting down my book and shooting them my most vitriolic glare.

"Dude!" said the effeminately dressed Black man around whom this family seemed to cluster. "Ya musta smoked ya'self some really nasty stuff, cuz it seems to be oozing outa yo eyeballs!" The others looked my way and nodded agreement.

Having not been heard by my eyes, I spoke with my words:

"Silence
Empty of all sound
Yet full
Full of opportunity to hear
Full of uncluttered windows to the world
Full of the gentleness of void
It does not penetrate brutishly
But flows soothingly into the soul
Massaging, eliciting, caressing, inviting
Luring into a different world

A world outside your own inner darkness
A world you robbed from me
When you stole
My silence."

One of the teenage girls sat wide-eyed with her mouth open.

"Wow!" she said softly. "That's so deep! I wish I were deep . . ."

"Space Princess," said a young Black girl who was part of the group, "ain't no way ya wanna be deep. If you was deep, ya would be totally lost to us, because ya would never find yo way out of ya own haid! Hell, we would have to send someone from Search and
Rescue into yo little brain, and girl, they've got enough to do already! Ain't that true, Emi-Lou?"

"'Fraid so, Camille" said a particularly attractive teenage girl to my left.

The girl who had been referred to as "Space Princess" furrowed her brow for a moment. "That's true . . ." she said quite seriously. Then her eyes widened. "Maybe I should buy a new hat instead."

Everyone looked her way seeking an understanding of her last statement, but as far as I could see, no one found so much as a clue. Still, the girl I now knew as Camille made an effort. "Girl, no one knows what's in that little noggin o' yours, but it's true at least a hat would cover it up, so you go for it."

"I know I don' understand so well dee English," said a Latina at the end of the table, "but I t'ink dees man he say for us to *cierra la boca*—how you say in Anglish?—shut up our mouths!"

I sighed in relief.

"The miracles of Lourdes and Turin

The water into wine, the river into blood, the dew-formed manna

The lame walking, the deaf speaking and the blind freed to see—

All these pale next to this:

I have been understood

By a woman."

"Okay, that's war!" said Camille, standing up. "One thing I know when I hear it is an insult to my gender. Maria, we sistas o' color need to get it on, 'cuz our white sistas here, they got no ghetto in 'em; so Maria, stand and deliver!"

The Black teen grabbed me by the collar and pulled me to my feet. Did I mention this was a rather LARGE young woman? And although Maria was not as large, she most certainly looked street-hardened. She also stood and glared at me with her arms crossed.

"All right you people," came a quiet, but authoritative voice from behind me, "I'm going to have to ask you to leave." A librarian.

"Hey!" said Camille, crossing her arms and looking at me. "We didn't start the fire, if ya know what I'm sayin'!"

"I don't care what you're saying, and I don't care who started it," said the tall, masculine-looking librarian. "All of you—out!"

My eyes widened and my heart raced.

"Cut out my heart
With a finely honed letter opener
Cast me o'er the rail
So I fall on my neck on hallowed marble banister
Hurl me through a shattering window to the streets below,
But do not,
do not,
do not
Exile me from my home while living,
From the friends gathered here
From the books
That warm and nurture
My soul."

Camille rolled her eyes and looked over at the librarian. "He talk like that all the time, I guess. Must be a disease er somethin'."

"Yeah, I've seen him before," said the librarian, speaking quietly. "And I don't care. All of you, out!"

I shivered.

The girl Camille had called "Emi-Lou" looked at me and gave me a half-smile. She leaned my way and whispered. "You know they let you check out books and take them with you, don't you?"

No poetry flowed, and my heart raced in panic. I would have to face a personal onslaught armed only with empty, impotent prose.

"Take them with me *where?*"

******

I'm standing on the top of the world
Though others might say
Only the top of the steps
Of the Multnomah County Library, Portland, Oregon,
Downtown Branch.

I see nothing, nothing, nothing
But the frigid bottom
To which I must now
Descend.

I had never had a need for a departure poem, and so this adaptation was the best I could do. A soft punch on the shoulder interrupted my thoughts. It was Camille.

"Yo, Dude! Look, my friends are all sayin', hell, like it's all our fault you out here, so maybe you should hang with us. I mean, if ya want to 'n all."

I looked over at the others. They didn't look hostile, but how could you tell with teenagers and others of today's unschooled masses?

"I don't know . . ."

Camille turned and walked away. "Okay, I tried—"

"Camille!" I was in such shock I didn't pick up which of the other teenage girls said this.

"I tried!" Camille protested. "What do ya want from me? I ain't beggin' no white dude to sit his white ass down next to mine, that's fer sure!"

The statement took me by surprise. Fear of rejection was something I was more used to feeling in my own heart than hearing in the words of another speaking about me.

"Out of the darkness
Of solitary cave
Out of the quiet of dripping water
And self-generated echo
You call me
And I creep

Slowly, cautiously
To the edge of threat
To risk hello
To risk abyss
For you."

Camille stared into my eyes and cocked her head slightly to the right, while narrowing her eyes to slits. "I'm not really sure," she said, "but I think I heard a 'yes' in there somewhere. What you think, Emi-Lou?"

The attractive teen came up and held out her hand. "Name's actually Emily." I shook it. "And maybe you can bring your books. Tell us all about them and your poetry?"

I had checked out two books and I held them close to my chest like a swaddled baby. I glanced down the library steps again at the street and foot traffic below. Everyone was going somewhere, most in a hurry. I think it was the speed that made my stomach tighten up. Or perhaps it was that, of all the many directions people were heading, I hadn't the least idea which one I might choose for that day. Normally, the only time I was out on the street was when the library was closed. On those occasions I tried to stay away from both the shadowy places which bred assault, and the even more frightening well-lit benches and plazas which bred conversation.

I looked back at Emily. She smiled a relaxed smile.

"These friends I have are bound

But not to me
I share them with you
If you brave to share yourself
Bravely, openly, tenderly
With me."

And so I descended from the top of the world.

I can't say I was comfortable. *When this family sits, where should I sit? When I could return to the library, would I return alone?* But most of all there was the conversation.

"How in the hell do you do that?" said Camille later that day after I had spoken.

"Do what?" I said tentatively, fearfully.

"How do ya jes—I don't know—jes spout off a poem, all neat and pretty like that?"

I could tell from her eyes she really wanted to know, but I had to suppress my initial lyrical reaction, because I knew it would not help. I took a deep breath and relaxed. I let the thought in my head come to my tongue slowly.

"What is difficult . . . isn't doing it," I said. "What is difficult for me is . . . is NOT doing it."

The wonder was, she understood.

The Emergency

From the corner of Fourth and Yamhill, from a cold sojourner's bench meant for giving brief respite to those in hectic journey, I looked up and saw my dreams fly by. Through the gaps formed by Portland skyscrapers, a silver bullet with wings made its way to an unseen horizon.

My heart ached as I watched.

I used to think I could see my horizon. It was effused with the color of the morning sun filtering past earth's dust and aerial refuse. Now all I seem to see is the dust and the refuse.

I was beautiful once. Men wanted to carry me off to the exotic places of the world, to the places where nothing was ever humdrum, where my green eyes sparkled with each morning, and my blond hair fluttered in each gust of refreshing wind. Who cared what the man wanted in return? He wouldn't get it. I could throw my head back and laugh, gently taking his arm, and guiding him where I wanted him to go, all the time letting him think he might get more. In that era, this strategy was enough.

In my dreams I was going to be a star—stage, screen, or the new medium of television, what did it matter? People around the world would see me and instantly know me, and they would want to please me. I had all it takes to be a star. I was beautiful. And yeah, I could also act, cry real tears on the stage, when necessary, that sort of thing.

Now men think I'm cute because I remind them of their grandma; my green eyes are clouded with cataracts; and my formerly blonde hair?—well, a sheep might be proud.

People call me "the Homeless Granny," but I'm not. I'm not homeless. Why do they assume? I have a home. I live in a little apartment on Ninth Avenue, which I share with cockroaches and rats. I suppose I should be grateful I'm not alone.

I got up from my bench and resumed my daily tour. You've got to keep moving, you know.

"Excuse me, please" I said in a soft, gentle voice to a young man in a snappy suit, "Could you spare me a dollar?" And I held out my hand. I saw the man's business-ready eyes soften and sparkle. I had hit my mark square on. He handed me a twenty. So, as you see, I still control the men.

Sometimes young people on the street wonder how I do it. They make their cardboard signs, some of which have a sob story about caring for hungry children; and some of which say, "I'll be honest; I just need a beer!" Some of their signs appeal to God's love and the Bible. None of these young people collect as much money as I do. Once I collected nearly $500 in one day.

Portland, Oregon, is a good town for doing what I do. The city has a nice downtown area, with good shopping, so people with money spend time there. And they have a rather liberal mindset—not as much of that Midwestern, judgmental, "get-a-job" way of thinking. They understand tough times. And even the ever-present rain helps. I am at my pathetic best when I am out in the cold rain, with it dripping down from my hair net into my saddest face.

I put all the money I collect into the bank and never check how much is in there. I never take money out; that way I know I will have it in case one day there is an emergency. That's the way my parents taught me. I confess I have not always done as my parents taught me, but I do now. I learned my lesson.

So, yesterday some sinister person put an eviction notice on my door. I walked to the manager's apartment and rang his bell. He emerged into the light of the hallway, not having even bothered to put on his shirt. His big pot belly hung over where, presumably, he had a belt; his five o'clock shadow had aged at least twenty-four hours; and the hair on his chest was only slightly less sparse and disheveled than those on his balding head. There was a time when I would have walked right past such a man without even acknowledging his existence.

"I'm sorry," I said in my gentlest voice, "but it seems someone put this on my door by mistake." And I handed him the eviction notice.

"No mistake, Mable," he said gruffly. "Ya haven't paid fer this month, ya know. Hell, ya only paid for half of the previous month. What do ya think, that this is some kind of free granny shelter? Ya don't pay, ya can't stay. That's all there is to it."

"But I'm old. It's not safe for me to sleep on the street."

"Then pay yer rent and we'll be fine."

I smiled my best smile. "Perhaps if you could wait until next Friday. That's when I get my Social Security check."

"And by then y'll need next month's rent, and y'll still be behind. Look, Mable, don't ya have some kids with money who can help ya out, er somethin'?"

I could feel my smile vanish from the inside out. "They have their own lives."

He grunted. "Okay, let's be honest here. I've seen ya out on the street. I mean, it's no business of mine, but I've seen ya panhandlin', and it seems to me ya do pretty well fer yerself in that department, huh? So jes turn some of that over, and we're good, okay?"

This man obviously didn't know my parents.

I left that man standing at the door without so much as a goodbye. I figured, if politeness doesn't work, don't be polite. Still, I wasn't sure what I was going to do. There was a time when men used to stand in line to rescue me from situations such as this one. Two of them even ended up marrying me, but I guess both tired of the job. I miss Eric. He was the good one.

So, now I was looking around the streets of Portland, searching for a man to rescue me. I saw the Peacemaker standing in front of the library. I didn't get why people on the street gave themselves such strange names: "the Peacemaker," "the Snake"—I even knew a man who called himself "the Pope of Yamhill." What's wrong with being proud of the name your parents gave you? My name is Mable; it's always been Mable; and will always be Mable. Sure, some people call me "the Homeless Granny" or even "Granny Moses," but you won't hear me using those names for myself. I'm proud of the name my parents gave me.

Anyway, I know the Peacemaker, and I'm nosy enough to know why he doesn't use his real name. I'm not telling *you*, though. Suffice it to say he felt he had things to make up for. What man doesn't? They are all driven by their hormones; a fuel which a smart, beautiful woman could pump, driving a man for her own little pleasure cruise until she was ready to park him beside the road wherever she wished. Had this man met me when I was young, well, he would have been my little joy ride, let me tell you. I sauntered nonchalantly in his direction.

"Good morning, Mister Peacemaker."

"Hey, Granny Moses."

I tightened my jaw, then relaxed it and smiled. "Mable would be fine, thank you."

He returned the smile. "Yes, of course . . . Mable."

I looked up at the bell tower of the Baptist Church across the street, and then visually surveyed the features of the other buildings on that corner, as if I were an out-of-towner, acquainting myself with the city for the first time. I had been to many other cities, of course, in my younger years. Few downtowns were as clean, as well-developed, or with as few eyesores as my hometown.

"Well, this is a nice city," I said. "I suppose if you are going to be ruthlessly thrown out on the street by your landlord, there could be worse places to have that happen."

"You're being evicted?"

I nodded. "I thought it was a mistake at first. I thought they would never do such a thing, but I was wrong."

"What are you planning to do?"

While I wasn't really tired, I walked slowly to a bus bench and sat down. I sighed deeply, and then, as if with great effort, looked up into his eyes.

"What am I going to do? Gracious sakes, I haven't the slightest idea! My family has lived in the Portland area for four generations, and I dare say nary a one of them has had to live in the street. My mother would roll over in her grave. And what will I do with my things? I have nice things: a music box I got in Switzerland, some charming Hummel figurines I bought in Germany, an old rocking chair that belonged to my grandmother—and this dress I am wearing! You see the lace on this dress? It's all hand-stitched and it's not meant to wear on the street, let me tell you! This is all just too overwhelming for me."

"Yeah, it's a difficult life out here," he said, mostly to himself it seemed. Then he looked more directly at me. "Was there something you were thinking I might do to help?"

"No, don't worry about me." That's what my mother would have said. "You have worries enough of your own, I am sure."

The Peacemaker slowly walked over and sat beside me on the bench. "There was a time when I could point you to some government or charitable agency that could help with rent, but with all the cutbacks—"

"Don't want a government handout."

The man sat quietly for a few moments and then his brow started to furrow. "You know, word on the street is that you pull in quite a bit of money from, well—handouts—not government ones, but, you know, people."

Why doesn't anyone understand about that money? If I used that money, it would be gone, and then what would I have left? People don't know how it was with my mother and father. They had gone through the Great Depression—this recent little economic blip paled in comparison—and they made it through by saving any little bit of money they could find. My sister and I would go to school without shoes rather than spending that little nest egg. My mother handmade all our clothing, including my little dress, which was just like the one I now wore, only smaller. My dad walked to work and never complained. He was glad he had work. And, no, I didn't understand why they did it myself when I was young. I left home when I was just sixteen years old, seeking my dream, and I never failed to find men who wanted to spend money on me. They wanted to. No one forced them. When I was getting older and worried about my fading beauty, I even married one of them and bore him children. I do believe I loved Eric. But he didn't understand me. When he didn't want to spend so much money on me, I found another man who would; and, no, Eric and the children didn't understand why I had left them. Okay, maybe I don't understand now either, but I did leave. And when the next one stopped wanting to spend money on me, I left him too.

Then my parents died. They didn't even warn me. They didn't warn me they were old and sick and wouldn't be around forever. I could have prepared if I had been warned. Maybe I would have heeded their words and followed their example earlier. When Eric also died, he left me as the target of the vitriolic hatred of two angry adult children, Franklin and Margaret, who at first eviscerated me with their cutting words, but who, when they tired of that, just turned and walked away forever. They haven't spoken to me in thirty years.

"Mable!" The Peacemaker was shaking my arm. "Mable, I'm trying to help, but you're not answering my questions."

"Yes, well . . . the money. I can't. I can't use that money. Don't ask me why, okay?"

The Peacemaker leaned back on the bench and scratched his head. "Okay . . . well, what about any other family members? Don't you have family who would be willing to help you?"

Everything around me was fading from my vision, and all I could see was the past. Still, this time I remembered I had a question to answer. "No. They all hate me. The living ones and the dead ones both—they all hate me. I have nowhere to go."

The Peacemaker got up and rubbed the stubble on his chin. I was no longer beautiful. But would my magic with men work just this one more time? He looked at me.

"Mable, what is your maiden name, and where were you born?"

"Harper. Mable Harper. I was born in my parents' house here in Portland, Multnomah County. Why are you—?"

The Peacemaker turned and ran up the library steps. "I'll get back to you as quickly as I can!"

In addition to being unfinished, my question was now also unanswered.

******

I sat on my bare mattress with its broken springs and looked out over my little studio apartment. Everything I owned was now packed and stacked up in one corner, and yet I had no idea of where it was going to go. I had to chuckle. As a child you're never thinking of where you are going next and how you are going to get there, because that is what the adults in your life are supposed to decide. Plan for the next step. Then you become an adult yourself, and you have all the plans laid out according to the blueprints provided by dreams in the fullness of their blossom. Mostly they never happen, but they are what fan your heart's flame and drive you forward. Then one day you wake up and realize those dreams have evaporated like a summer rain; but it's not all that important because what happens next has nothing to do with those dreams anyway. Someone else tacks your tomorrow on your door. You're a child again, waiting for someone else to show you what's next.

Someone knocked on my door.

Now, I suppose it would be helpful in telling my story to say that people just never knock on my door. I'm afraid I don't have many friends, and the few I have wouldn't just drop by to see how I am doing. They all have troubles of their own. And, yes, the apartment manager does knock when he is coming for the rent, or once in a blue moon to fix something I have asked to be fixed; but, of course, I wasn't expecting him to fix any of the many things which needed to be fixed, since he wouldn't do so before kicking me out on the street. So, I figured he had come earlier than expected to do his dirty business.

I was not in a rush to go to the door.

The knock came again.

If I don't go to the door, maybe I won't have to leave.

The next knock rattled the door frame. Had my Hummel figurines still been on their little shelf, they probably would have fallen off.

"Mabel! Are you in there? Are you okay?"

The voice was not the apartment manager's voice. I got up, walked over and put my ear against the door.

"Who is it?" I knew my voice was weak and I wondered if it could be heard on the other side of the door.

"It's me, Mable. The Peacemaker."

I opened the door.

I hadn't realized how dark it was in my apartment. Now, as I opened the door the hall lights framed two visitors in an aura. TWO visitors. The one on the right I knew to be the Peacemaker, even though, because of that aura, I might not have recognized him without his previous self-identification. The one on the left was a woman. As my eyes adjusted, she looked much more familiar, and my heart palpitated.

"Hello, Mother."

"Margaret! I, uh—"

"Are you angry with me, Mable?" asked the Peacemaker. "I guess I should have cleared it with you first, but I had to try this."

"How did you—?"

"Find her? Computer search. Anyway, she paid the rent for you, Mable. I thought you should know as soon as possible."

My daughter stood quietly in the doorway, glassy-eyed and quivering.

"You didn't need to do that, Margaret. I, uh . . . I have not been a good mother."

"I did need to do it, Mother," she said, now looking down at the floor. "For lots of reasons, I guess. I'm an addict. And a Christian. A Christian addict. Anyway, I've been really angry with you, and I've hated you. Thought hateful thoughts." She looked up at me now, but I could tell it was with much effort. "I'm in recovery now. Doing well. I have been clean and sober for over a year, and I'm working for Microsoft up in Bellevue. Anyway, I'm on Step Eight, and the *Big Book* says I should make amends to those who I've wronged."

"You've wronged me?" I said, barely able to get the words out. "No, no! I'm the one—"

"Yes, but I'm also the one, Mother!" My daughter's face now showed some anger, but it was not clear whether the anger was at me or at herself. "I've known for a long time that I should forgive, but I couldn't—wouldn't. It took me thirty years. You just didn't know, Mother! You didn't know how what you did affected Frankie and me. You were weak, and all you could see was your own hurting, that's all. So—"

"My dear, I don't deserve forgiveness."

"None of us do, Mother. None of us do."

I looked back into my darkened apartment. "I would invite you in, but—"

"I can't, Mother. I mean, to be honest, I have the time, but I can't. I've done all I can do right now. Perhaps another time."

By the time I turned around to face her, she was running down the hallway.

******

I was talking to my daughter again. Twice by phone later that week and once again the following week when she came by and sat down in my old, dingy apartment. She even said that Franklin was working up the courage to come by as well. It was like a dream. I kept wanting to thank the Peacemaker, but he disappeared like the Masked Man of television long ago, and I didn't see him again. All I knew was, I had a daughter and one day I might have a son again, and the world looked different. The rains still came down—it was Portland—but the sky didn't seem as gray.

I think I looked different as well. Probably not as sad. I liked that, but it didn't help me get money from people. It got so bad I had to practice making my "sad Granny" face just to get anything at all. I was having a difficult time finding motivation for my act.

I also discovered I was looking at people on the street who I knew would never give me anything, looking at them and smiling for no reason. One day in the early morning when I hadn't been able to sleep, I walked all the way to the Skidmore Fountain. All around me homeless people were still asleep in their sleeping bags. I knew some were drunks and addicts, and normally I looked right past them, but this time I thought how Margaret might have been in a place like this before her recovery. She had told me she had been on the street for five years not too long ago, before she got herself together and got a job. As I looked at these people now, tears came to my eyes.

Then I saw a couple of young kids, teenagers really, sleeping on asphalt under the bridge. I found myself walking in their direction. The morning was cold, and I could see the young girl shiver. The young man curled his arm around her in a seemingly futile effort to keep her warm. I surveyed their situation and all I could see that might belong to them was an old radio, or I guess they call it a "boom box," a few feet away. The young girl's nose was running, and she coughed in her sleep. That's when the young man woke up and looked at me. He smiled.

"Hey, Granny Moses."

"My name is not . . . oh, well."

The young woman woke up and looked at me also, but she didn't speak. She sniffled a little and then reached around down inside her bag. She came out with a dollar bill and handed it to me.

"Oh, no!" I said. "You need that more than I."

"But your face!" she said. "It's so sad! I can't stand to see such a sad, old face!"

At least I had found my motivation for my "sad Granny" act.

Later that morning, I strode confidently past several businessmen in suits, down Yamhill and across Pioneer Square. I only paused a moment to watch the tourists and shoppers lined up at the food kiosks, or heading toward the mall. Then I continued on my way over to Fifth Avenue. I stopped briefly at the door. I couldn't remember if I had been in my bank since opening my account, now over five years ago. I hadn't wanted people on the street to see me depositing money, so I had mailed in my deposits. I went through the door and walked up to one of the tellers, a nice-looking young woman with a big smile.

"Excuse me," I said, speaking so quietly the young woman leaned my way and cocked her right ear towards me, "but would you mind helping me with my account?"

"Certainly. How can I help?"

"I would like to withdraw my money now."

"Certainly. Could I have your name and account number, please?"

I gave her my name and the number, and she typed the information into the computer. When she found what she was looking for, her eyes widened, and she shifted those eyes in my direction.

"I'm sorry, but did you want to withdraw ALL of your money?"

A vision of the young couple asleep by Skidmore Fountain merged with a memory of another young couple long ago.

"Yes," I said. "I am afraid there is an emergency."

The Invitation

I've been called "Candy" for so long that I have forgotten if I ever had another name, or if I did, what it was. I seem to remember the name "Lucy," but that might not be my real name. It's just that I'm Asian and some of my friends thought I looked a little like Lucy Liu, so that may have been why they called me "Lucy."

Or maybe my name was "Amy. " I really can't remember.

Still, "Candy" is appropriate. Candy lures you in with a show of sweetness, gives you a quick high, drops you quickly, and leaves you with nothing but a craving for more. That's me, and if you don't like it, then frankly I don't give a shit.

Of course, in my case, the sweetness is artificial sweetness. I hate those girls all the other girls call "sweet." Dotting their 'i's with little hearts and putting happy faces on all of their communications. *Ah! Isn't that sweet!* Smiling and giggling, playing with puppies and saying nice things about people even when the person isn't worth shit. *Ah! Isn't she sweet!* Makes me want to vomit.

Of course, the men I do business with like the name Candy. It sounds more like a treat than a real girl. No girl named Candy is going to challenge your masculinity. No girl named Candy is going to expect a commitment from you. No girl named Candy is going to expect more from you than that you pay for your candy.

It's not a bad life, though. I don't have to go out on the street a lot because I market myself on the internet. When I do go out on the street, it's when it's not raining, and I want to flaunt what I've got before men too timid to go searching for it. I hang out around Pederson's store a lot. Men looking for girlie magazines down there get a jolt when an Asian hottie with real curves smiles at them. They're all like *Oh, my God! What do I do now?* I like to brush one of my boobs against them while I'm reaching for some stupid fan magazine, and when they notice, I give them my smile again. Pretty soon they're scrambling to get to their ATM, when all they thought they were doing was sneaking a quick peek at some porn and maybe buying a pack of cigarettes. I love it!

I'm different with the street people. I don't mean the other women of my profession, though some of them I'm almost friends with. We put up with the same shit and all. I mean the people who live on the street because they have nowhere else to go. Sometimes I even give them money. I mean, that old Homeless Granny—who could refuse to give her money? Saddest face I've ever seen. Reminds me of my own grandmother, even though she's not Asian.

Most of the men on the street can't afford me, of course. Well, except for that guy who calls himself the Peacemaker. He came to me a couple of years ago, just after he had lost his job. He's avoided me ever since. Guilt, I guess.

People on the street are more real than the men who are my customers. My customers are all pretending, which is okay, because that is what I am doing too. I have gotten very good at pretending—pretending affection, pretending to show empathy for a guy in his empty little marriage, pretending orgasms. And they pretend they're really hot studs and it's not about the money.

People on the street know who they are. They know the dreams they had as children have all crumbled, and most of them know it's their own damn fault. They know their own insignificance, that nothing in this world is about them, that maybe even God looks past them as they walk along. For me, they are the fallen angels of a sick and broken world.

Of course, some see *me* as a fallen angel in a sick and broken world. Okay, whatever.

So, as I said, I do market myself on the internet, principally through this site that advertises to "men looking for women" called hornycoeds.com. Yeah, like I was ever a coed! Didn't even graduate from high school! Anyway, I got this really weird message from a man who said right up front he was a minister of a church, and his church would very much like it if I would come to their church and share what my life was like as "a young call girl/prostitute/woman of the night"—and *what did I like to be called?* He said they were a progressive, non-judgmental Christian church and would pay me for my time in accordance with my "normal fees." Really.

I was a little curious about how they found me out. Let's see, hornycoeds.com. Surely that wouldn't have clued them in. The picture was of me in a cheerleader's outfit where, as I jumped up, it showed my crotchless panties and my halter top with a wardrobe malfunction. Nothing sus about that. Instead of "long walks on the beach," I listed as my turn ons "frolicking naked on the beach and taking a pounding in the waves." Now that I re-read that, maybe it wasn't as subtle as I originally thought.

So, I said, "What the hell?" and I called them. The first thing I did was to read to the minister the law about what constituted *entrapment*, you know, just in case. He said that wouldn't be happening. Then I said, "Candy." And he said, "Excuse me?" And I said, "You asked in the email what I liked to be called, and so I said 'Candy.'" He meant what I would like my profession to be called.

"Yeah, you know," he said, "I mean, housewives and househusbands like to be called 'domestic engineers,' and what we used to call 'secretaries' now like to be called 'administrative assistants;' stewardesses are now 'flight attendants' and, so . . .?"

"Queen of Fuck."

"Yeah, you're pulling my leg now, aren't you?"

"No, but I suppose I would if you paid me."

He was quiet.

"Okay," I said, "'Erotic Attendant'? Is that taken?"

"Uh, no . . . I guess not."

"It kinda goes with the others you were talking about, so, yeah."

The whole thing was a little bit scary to me, so I think I was trying to turn him off to the idea, but he didn't let go.

"So, do you have any questions?"

"Yeah—why?"

"Why what?"

The word "why?" pretty much summed it up for me, but I guess my profession had trained me to be cooperative with men. "Why are you asking me to do this? I mean, call me crazy, but I always thought church people wanted to avoid women in my profession . . . well, at least in public."

"As I said, we are a progressive church. We see ourselves as an inclusive fellowship. We were talking about how Jesus went around with prostitutes, and we thought it would be good if we met one and found out a little about her."

"You needed a token Jesus whore?"

"Well . . . we weren't thinking—"

I just should have bailed at that moment. I mean, I certainly didn't need church people looking at me and wondering what "went wrong" with my life. And I really didn't need to stand in for all whoredom so someone could have their little devotional moment feeling close to Jesus. So, why didn't I?

"Okay, I'll do it."

After I hung up, I thought I should have asked if he wanted references from other ministers who I have done business with, but it's just as well—he might not have appreciated the humor.

It's not like I had never been to a church. When I was little my mother used to take me to a Chinese Baptist Church in San Francisco. I liked it. But as I grew up and got out on my own, what I experienced there just didn't seem to fit the world. Oh, I did go back a time or two in Portland after I had gotten into the business. One was a church that didn't have any crosses, had Starbucks coffee in their lobby, and seemed to go out of their way to *not* talk about Jesus. I left there thinking *What the fuck kind of church is it that doesn't talk about Jesus?* So, I went to a different church with the name "Baptist" in it, because I figured at least they would talk about Jesus, and they did. They talked about a Jesus who was coming back to judge all the people like me and throw them into hell, while taking all the good, righteous people like them into heaven. I noticed at least three of my customers, all trying to look the other way.

I also tried a Catholic church, because that was about as different from Baptist as I could think of. I liked some things. It all seemed so mysterious and holy. They talked about Jesus, and they also talked about Mary. I liked the Mary part. I could relate to Mary. A young girl, pregnant, who no one understood. Been there, done that. What I couldn't relate to were the confessionals. No way I was going to talk about my life to a man I couldn't even see. I finally decided church just wasn't for me.

So now I had volunteered to become a featured guest at a church, and all that kept running through my mind was *What were you thinking, Madame Shit-for-Brains*? So, the date was a week away and I decided to just throw myself into my work and try and forget about it.

My clients love it when I throw myself into my work.

After three days and nights of jumping, bumping, and humping half the male population (and yes, some of the female population) of downtown Portland, I just had to pause and take a breather. In my profession, your body can take a lot of violations, but it's not so easy when you allow your comfort zone to be violated, as I had. I thought about just bagging it, but I have a real thing against going back on my word. Maybe people don't realize that about me. They think that if you're in my line of work, you don't have any principles at all. Not true.

So, I was in a dilemma. When I find myself in a dilemma, I go to the people I know who have to solve dilemmas all the time as a consequence of their life situation—homeless street people.

I first looked for the Peacemaker because I know he gives good advice to people all the time, but as soon as he saw me smiling at him, he turned and hustled off the other way. Shit, he was in such a hurry he nearly ran in front of the MAX train.

Well, he's not the only person I know on the street. When I talked to the Snake he tried to shoot me with somebody's umbrella. Must have been off his meds. I talked to Cole, and he just stared at me glassy-eyed, repeating, "You want advice from ME? You want advice from ME? You want—" Oh, well, what the hell. You get the idea.

So, I decided that talking to men about this problem, even men off the street, was like talking to the family dog. They look like they're listening, but really, their drool just gets in the way.

I saw Crazy Jane, the bag lady, and I knew she at least went in churches a lot, mostly to get free meals. I didn't expect too much, because most of the time she's too caught up in conversation with the demons inside her head to let herself get distracted by any other interactions. Still, what she said made me think.

"Beware!" she said, after I told her my situation. "Beware!" she repeated, with her eyes scanning first to the right and then to the left. By the time she said the third "Beware!" I was almost ready to run in front of a MAX train myself. Then she went on: "People who want to get to know you! That's who you should beware of! No good can come of that!" Then she grabbed the handle of her shopping cart and sped off down the sidewalk, as if she thought *I* was the one trying to get to know *her*.

I must have stood there twenty minutes, arguing with myself over whether or not she was right. Maybe that's why I have such a tough time remembering whether or not Candy is my real name.

I gave it another shot. Emily was a teenage girl I had met over by Pederson's. I found she had been through some tough stuff and had become pretty street smart, and yet I seemed to remember she also had some church experience as well. I found her down at Pioneer Square, sitting on the concrete steps with her street family. They're mostly female, except for James who is gay, and that doesn't count, as far as that dumb drooling stuff I mentioned is concerned. I sat down next to Emily.

"Oh, good, Ms. Candy is here!" said James. "Now we can finally get some attention from the cops. I've really been missin' havin' them dudes kick around my little Black ass!"

I tried to ignore his sarcasm and get to the purpose of my visit, but Maria, a Latina immigrant, was too quick to the trigger.

"I no need dos guys, dee' cops! *Por favor,* you go away now, okay?"

"Come on you guys!" I said. "You know me, and you know the cops leave me alone. Unless, of course—"

"Yeah, girlfriend!" said Camille, a young Black girl I had talked to on occasion, "It's that damn 'Unless, of course . . .' I 'no need'! Unless, of course they after a little action that day theyselves! Yeah, I 'no need' that shit. I no need your cute little Asian ass wigglin' around in front of all the dudes! I get enough competition from pretty little Emi-Lou here."

"Me?" injected Emily. "I don't—"

"Shut up! Shut up! Shut up!" I underlined the words with my most intimidating face, the one I use with guys who were trying to stiff me. "I just need a little advice, then I'm gone, okay?" I told them my story, and then looked to Emily, since she is the one I had come to see primarily. But, of course, she wasn't the one who responded first.

"Hey, Lucy Liu, what the hell you been smokin'?" said Camille. "Agreein' to go to some uppity white church so they can feel sorry for ya and act all superior an' all? I mean, if you feelin' guilty, and need someone to whip yo little ass, then—"

"Do *I* have a little ass?" This question had come from the white teenager everyone called the Space Princess. She twisted around inspecting her derriere. "I have little boobs, I know that. I heard they're going to make a Barbie doll with little boobs. But you know what doll I used to like? Raggedy Ann! I don't remember if Raggedy Ann had a little ass, but she didn't have boobs. She had button eyes, though. What do you think it would be like to try to see through button eyes?"

"MY ADVICE, PLEASE!" I stood up and discovered I was yelling, so I toned it down a couple of notches. "I just want to know what Emily thinks, but if any of the rest of you have an opinion—on my question, not my boob and ass size—then I would be glad to hear from you also, AFTER I hear from Emily. So, Emily—"

"Do it."

"You think I should do it."

"Yeah."

"Even though it's got me scared shitless?"

Emily shrugged. “I can’t remember a time when I wasn’t scared of something. If I didn’t do what I was scared of, I wouldn’t do anything at all.”

“Really?”

“When I go ahead and do something that scares me, it makes me that much freer. So, yeah.”

Finally, some sense.

******

I had forgotten how intimidating the outside of some church buildings can be. This one looked like a castle, built of huge impregnable stones, with turrets rising high above me, and a steeple rising even higher. The front entrance had a gate of iron bars, which I guessed had only recently been pulled open, with iron bars also across the lower windows.

The only thing missing was a moat with crocodiles.

I’m not sure why this church wanted to scare me off any more than it already did, but my thoughts kept going back to Emily’s words. Why had I accepted them so easily as being true? Sometimes there’s plenty of reasons to be scared and back away. If I see a John with a wild look in his eyes, or someone who starts calling me vile, hateful names, or starts spouting judgmental scripture at me, I get out of there as fast as I can, and I do not even hesitate. I’ve had friends in the business who’ve been sliced and diced and on the five o'clock news for not being careful in those kinds of situations.

Still, something told me this situation was different, and that Emily was probably right.

An elderly couple met me at the door. They were both very sweet. She took my hand and held it tightly as she looked into my eyes and smiled the most genuine smile I had seen in a long time. She told me that I didn't need to be nervous, because the people who were there were very good, caring people; and I told her I wasn't nervous, which by then was only a little lie because her presence had made me feel that much better. Her name was Gladys.

Gladys' husband was Eric, and he also gave me a great smile, although he seemed to struggle a little with keeping his eyes on mine. Emily and her street family had helped me pick out something to wear, and although it was more modest than what I normally wear, I was showing some cleavage, and I knew even a little of my cleavage was an eye magnet for men. He must have sensed his own struggle because he quickly apologized, saying he ought to know better how to behave around attractive young women, and would I forgive him? He then managed to keep his smiling eyes on mine for several seconds before I realized he really did want an answer. *Would I forgive him?*

"Oh . . . of course!"

Gladys put her arm around my shoulder. "The man's an animal, but I love him!" she said with a laugh. "Come this way."

Eric stood on my other side and offered me his arm, as if he were escorting the two of us to a wedding. I smiled and took it.

There were about forty people in the hall where everyone had gathered. Most of them were older men and women. The younger women were all in a little circle, looking my way and periodically bending their heads toward each other and whispering. I decided that was okay. I had been the new girl in school before.

There were two young men in the group. They also stood together, but the way their mouths hung open, it was obvious they were neither talking nor planning on talking. I looked their way and smiled, and they both blushed and turned away.

The older people were all moving in our direction. I was surprised that Gladys and Eric were not the only ones who seemed welcoming. I met Charles and Wilma, Eunice, Karl and Geraldine, Priscilla, and a lesbian couple, Sarah and Charlotte. There were others too who were equally welcoming, but whose names I do not remember.

Gladys explained that we would eat first, and I remembered the same thing from the church of my childhood in San Francisco: weekday programs always began with a potluck where there was lots of good food, after which the kids could play. I loved that part. I knew in this case I would not be given time to play, but still the memory gently massaged my spirit.

I felt a hand touching my shoulder from behind. I turned and saw the face of one of the young women who had been talking together. She was obviously nervous and uptight, as she shuffled a little, and her eyes darted around the room.

"Hi, I'm Kayla," she said. Then after a pause she finally looked me in the eyes. "I'm afraid I'm really not sure how to talk to you, but I wanted you to know that I want to try." She motioned toward the older people still standing nearby. "I mean, like, these are beautiful people, their love is genuine, their faith is awesome, and I really want to be like them, so I hope you will just give us all a chance to get to know you." She held out her hand.

I looked into her eyes for a few seconds. They were beautiful green eyes, and they were tearing up a little, as if she had just made a move toward reuniting a broken friendship. I took her hand, but my mouth only trembled. We shook hands. Then she motioned toward one of the tables.

"My friends and I are all eating here, and we would love for you to hang with us during dinner . . . I mean, if you like—"

I looked back at Gladys and Eric, thinking they would be a safer option. "It's your choice," said Gladys, "and we would be happy whichever way you choose."

I wondered if I ever had any of the young women's boyfriends as a customer. I even wondered if Kayla's hospitality was a trap, like being invited to the popular girls' table back in high school. I had that happen once. They told me that if I ever even talked to one of their boyfriends, they would tear my hair out by the roots. Then they dumped my lunch tray on the floor.

I remembered Emily's words. *Doing what scares you makes you freer!* I remembered Crazy Jane's words. *Beware the people who want to know you!*

Be free!

Beware!

Be free!

Beware!

Kayla touched me on the arm, and I could see the question raised again in her eyes. My heart was racing. Still that heart was also telling me which side it wanted to win.

"Okay. I would like to sit with you," I said.

"And, I'm sorry," said Kayla, "but what was your name again?"

"My name?" My heart kicked into overdrive.

"Yes, please, unless that is too personal?"

I took a deep breath. I focused on slowing my heart rate. I tensed and relaxed my shoulders. Then from my face I let escape the biggest smile I had smiled since childhood.

"Mary," I said. "My name is Mary!"

And, I don't know, maybe it was.

The Mission

When the explosion came, I was the only one who was ready. Oh, I'm not braggin' or trying to make out like I'm better'n everyone else. I had been trained, and they hadn't. Simple as that.

"Take cover!"

The explosion had come from behind, from an empty-looking building we had just passed. *We shoulda checked it out—my fault! I shoulda said something*. But now there could be no "shouldas"; there was only the cover in some bushes just ten meters ahead, and I ran for it, low to the ground as we had done so many times in boot camp. Holding tight to my AK-47, I dove and lled and then twisted around to aim my weapon in the direction of our attackers. But there in my sight stood my buddy in his civvies, stooped over, with his hands on his hips and his mouth wide open.

"Snake, what the HELL are you doin'? That was a fuckin' truck backfire!"

I wasn't convinced. Nothing in this world is what it seems. I had learned that time and time again. Women and old codgers, looking like ordinary people living their lives—and carrying bombs.

That eight-year-old Iraqi girl I killed. She probably was, even though I never could check. I just shot her and moved on. And now they're telling me that this was a truck backfire?

"I need to secure that building, Cole! It's a nesting place for Saddam's Sunni militants!"

Cole looked back at the building. "That building? Hell, that's an old warehouse they're turning into upscale condos. This is the fuckin' Pearl District, Snake! Portland, Oregon. Now put down that old walkin' stick you're pointing and get over here. You're makin' a scene and embarrassin' me!"

Okay, first of all, there was no way I was surrendering my weapon. But Cole was my buddy, standing by my side when others wouldn't. I owed him, so I didn't make any snide comments. I got back up on my feet and stealthily approached the building in question. A brick shell, with the windows knocked out long ago, probably from other nearby explosions. Most of the windows were covered with plywood. Except I found one they had missed. I grabbed hold of the sill and jumped up and through the opening. Two shadows to my left caught my attention, and I swung my weapon around, pointing and holding it steady. Two men in suits emerged into the sunlight streaming through my window. Probably U.S. reconstruction contractors. I lowered my weapon.

"God, just what we need in here, another homeless bum!" said one of the suits.

I think he was talking about me.

"Get your ass out of here!" said the other. "When we're done with this you won't be able to afford to rent a closet in this place."

Yeah, that's the way it was with these civvy contractors. Hell, we were here fighting for freedom, and they thought it was freedom for them to screw everybody over. I would have puked right there, but I knew I had to stay alert. I raised my weapon toward them once more.

"God, just what we fuckin' need," said the shorter one. "Isn't this why they are supposed to give them exit counseling, so they don't go all postal on us? What if that were a real gun?"

Cole stuck his head through the window opening. "Come on, Snake! The building is secure. We're needed in Baghdad."

When my country needed me, I never hesitated. I gave one of the suits a friendly parting nudge, sending him to the floor, then I vaulted through the window opening. Cole took hold of my arm.

"Hey, Snake, how long since you last took your meds?"

I stared at him. *Why isn't he telling me about the mission in Baghdad?*

"You remember the medication you're supposed to take, don't you?"

In the back of my mind, I remembered something about medication. I just couldn't remember where it was or why I was taking it. The next thing I remember, Cole was frisking me, and he discovered a partially full plastic bottle in my left front pants pocket.

"We shouldn't be doing that stuff when we're out on assignment!"

"It's okay," Cole said. "I'm the medic, remember?"

I didn't, but I took his word for it. When you're fighting in a part of the world where there are so few you can trust, you have to trust the buddy who fights alongside you. You just have to, that's all there is to it. So, when he gave me the pill, I took it.

******

I don't remember when I came to Portland. Or why. I wasn't raised here. I was raised as an Army brat and lived almost everywhere in this country except Portland: Tacoma, Washington; Junction City, Kansas; Fort Leonard Wood in Missouri; Fort Bragg in North Carolina; Fort Bliss down in Texas. *Did I miss any?* Who knows? Anyway, I never lived in Portland, because Portland doesn't have an Army base.

Hell, maybe that's why I came.

Whatever. When I'm on my medication, the whole world is "whatever." It's like how Portland is nine months out of the year: gray skies blending in with the gray buildings, which rise above the gray lives of the four or five hundred thousand people who live here.

Which is worse: too much that is gray, or too much that rises up and scares the hell out of you? I'm really not sure, but that is the question I spend most of my day thinking about.

I wish people wouldn't look at me like I'm crazy all the time. They do, you know. Some days more than others. Today people were catching hold of me with their eyes and not letting go until I was clearly past them, as if they expected me to pull a knife on them at any moment. It was enough to make me wish I had one to pull. Hell, if I weren't on my medication, I'm sure that I could have imagined one.

I took my normal walk from my rightfully claimed sleeping spot near the Skidmore Fountain down First Avenue toward Pioneer Square, but this morning for some reason I detoured through the Pearl District. Hell, I don't know why, maybe it was because I wanted to imagine I belonged there in the middle of all those high-priced condos and swank restaurants. Of course, in my gut I knew I really didn't. You see, that's the thing about those of us who have fought for freedom: we get the fight, while those who successfully avoided it get the benefits. But I don't want to talk about that.

That's when I walked past this old brick warehouse, perhaps the last one in the Pearl District that hadn't been turned into something expensive. I stopped in front of it. I felt this anxiety inside me about the building, but I didn't know where it came from. There was one ground-level window which had not been boarded over, and I walked up to it. I had a strong sense of *déjà vu.*

I crawled into the window and sat with one leg inside the building and one leg out. Inside the building were stacks of lumber, decorative stone, and brick. A man in a suit emerged from the shadows and looked my way.

"Shit! Are you back here again?" He came my way waving a T square like a sword. "I thought we told you to stay the fuck out of here!"

I held out my right hand. "They call me the Snake. Fought in the Persian Gulf. Just wanted a look-see at the progress my efforts made possible."

The man stopped a couple of feet away, and stared at my proffered right hand like he thought it was holding a dead rat.

"The Snake, huh? How come 'the Snake'?"

I let my hand drop. "'Cuz I would come into a building like this filled with hostiles, and my buddies said I would slink around corners like a snake, checkin' the place out. Name kinda stuck when I came back to the States."

He looked around nervously, avoiding my eyes now. "Yeah . . . well, like we said before, you can't come in here, okay? We're getting it ready for renovation. This window should have been covered a long time ago."

I nodded. "So, I came here before?"

He looked at me like I was from another planet. "Yeah. Just yesterday! Don't you remember?"

I surveyed the property one more time and then looked him in the eye. "You're welcome!"

I swung my leg out and dropped back to the sidewalk. I had taken three steps before I heard his “Thank you!”

******

An old woman saluted me once. Yeah, I was on the street and not even in my uniform, but there she was saluting me, so I saluted back. I suppose it’s possible she met me before, when I wasn’t on my meds. I didn’t get her name. People said she thought she was Judy Garland er somethin’. I didn’t care. She seemed happy, and I haven’t seen much happiness. When you see someone who is happy you get a sense that maybe you can be happy too. For me, happiness would be living in a world that was neither gray nor frightening, and doing it without having to take medication. Wouldn’t that be somethin’?

I followed the old woman around for a while, trying to learn from her, I guess. As I did, I was getting a stronger and stronger sense that someone was followin’ *me*. In Iraq you do have to develop an extra sense to survive, a sense which tells you when there is someone around who wants to do you harm. I had that sense, and it was setting off alarm bells in my admittedly traumatized little brain.

Whenever I turned around, someone would disappear into the shadows.

I sometimes wonder what I would do if I were no longer frightened of something. Would I know how to react? I don't really know. The Judy Garland lady didn't seem frightened of anything. She lived on the street like all the rest of us and never seemed to look behind her.

Going through life frightened slowly wears you down, and after a while you don't care anymore. You start to wonder, *What that's chasing me could be worse than what has hold of me right now?*

Cole pulled me down on a bench and sat beside me. "Taking your medication?"

"Yes."

"Are you sure?"

"Of course. If I weren't taking my medication, I wouldn't remember I have medication." I pretty much had him on that one.

"Then why are you so jumpy? Hell, I look at you and I start lookin' for a fuckin' foxhole myself!"

"Someone is followin' me."

"Someone is always followin' you, Snake! Hell, ever since I met you—and I gotta tell ya I'm really beginning to regret the day—someone has been followin' you. Why don't you just let 'em find you and have it out?"

"I'm thinkin' they're trying to catch me with my guard down."

Cole rolled his eyes. "What in the hell would they want from you? No perv rapist would have ya—you're ugly as sin."

"Maybe they think I have my VA disability money on me."

"You get a VA disability check?"

"Yeah. Post-traumatic stress disorder is a disability. So, yeah."

Cole looked at me like he was gazing at a slice of prime rib. "Okay, now I'm thinkin' of muggin' ya myself!"

It was my turn to roll my eyes. "I don't have it on me. I have a kid up in Seattle. Most of it I send to him. The rest I keep in an account and only get some when I really need it."

Cole pulled out a cigarette and lit it. "I sure as hell know about that shit. Except I have no idea where my kid is. I ain't got no VA disability money to send to him neither."

We sat there watching people walk up and down the sidewalks of Yamhill Street. Everyone was going somewhere but us. I noticed one young girl, really pretty, who was walking along with a cell phone seemingly glued to her ear and looking like she was in some kind of frickin' power-walking marathon. She was wearing a sexy tight miniskirt, but that didn't seem to inhibit her walking speed any. I sat there trying to decide if I was more frustrated because she was hot and made me horny, or because she was so much younger than I and seemed to have some high-paying job and urgent tasks to accomplish, neither of which I had at present. Either way my preacher Grandpa would have said getting all worked up about it was just like chasing the wind.

I looked over at Cole. He was eyeballing the same girl, and his face was shadowed in anger.

"You know that old Judy Garland lady?" I asked.

"Yeah, what about her?"

"Why do you think she seems so happy when we're not?"

Cole bristled. "Well, for one thing she's not an old dude havin' to look at hot young women they can't have. Hell, she's ninety years old—the sex gods figure they've tormented her enough and they leave her the hell alone."

"Gotta be more than that."

"Yeah, well, maybe she's got religion er somethin'."

"I've gotten religion four times down at the Union Gospel Mission. Hasn't helped me none, though."

Cole swatted my arm and pointed a finger at me. "Don't you go puttin' down religion, ya hear?"

"What's it to you? I know I've seen you down there, but if there's one dude who I know doesn't have religion, I'm sorry, but I gotta say—"

"I go there lots of times!" he said, raising his voice so much that several passersby glared down at us. "But no, I've never come to Jesus—well, not recently anyway."

I leaned back on the bench and tried to act nonchalant. "Why not?"

He sat there shaking his head for a while. Then he closed his eyes and slid down on the bench. "God, I don't think even Jesus would want a shithead like me."

"You're probably right," I said. He looked at me indignantly. "Hey, me too!" Then I started laughing, at first just a little, but soon I was so out of control I had slipped off the bench onto the sidewalk. A couple of men who had to step around me looked down at me like I was drunk.

Cole sat beside me on the sidewalk. Now all the passersby were having to detour around us, which pissed off a number of them, but we didn't care.

"Next time you're thinkin' about reminding me about my medication," I said, "just don't. I think if I'm going to be runnin' around scared of somethin', it's better if it's just my imagination."

Cole nodded. Then he seemed to be thinking about something really hard, and he turned towards me. "If you don't want it, can I have it?"

"No."

"That's it? 'No.' No explanation."

'That's right. Just 'no.'"

I wasn't sure at first how long the Peacemaker had been standing there. But as he sat down on the bench Cole and I had vacated, I got a clearer idea.

"You know, guys, we would all be in pretty bad shape if Jesus didn't take in shitheads."

"The hell, you say!" Cole just shook his head and laughed.

"Peacemaker, how come you don't let anyone know your real name?" I asked. "You and that Judy Garland lady, the same way. Seems to me if the two of you had it as together as ya act like, ya wouldn't mind letting people know your real name."

"Yeah," chimed in Cole, "like Snake here. He come out of his mama's privates so slick that his mama, she named him 'Snake' right then and there."

Don't think Cole didn't irritate the hell outta me.

"I ain't pretendin' I'm all full of the wisdom of life and all," I said. "I don't tell my name, because I got something to be scared of. What you got to be scared of, Peacemaker?"

"It's not about being scared," he said. "I'm not hiding my real name; I just decided on a different one because I wanted to be different than I used to be. I had a regular name once, and I just pissed on it and brought it to shame, along with everyone else who held the name before me. When I decided to be a new person, I decided on a new name, that's all there is to it. You know, your *real* name isn't necessarily the name your momma or your daddy gave you."

"That's good," said Cole. "'Cuz my momma and daddy really did call me 'shithead.'"

"What about the Judy Garland lady?" I asked.

"I call her 'The Dancing Girl.'"

"More like 'Dancing Old Lady,'" said Cole.

"No," insisted the Peacemaker, "when she dances, she is a girl."

Even with all that talk and company, I was beginning to get that antsy feeling again, and I turned around quickly. As I did, I noticed a young white dude in an old, faded, blue down jacket with a hole in one elbow looking at me. As I noticed him, he turned quickly toward the window of Peterson's convenience store where I knew you could see their extensive porno magazine selection. An older Black dude edged up to him on the other side and whispered something in his ear.

Suddenly it seemed like the whole world was looking at me, wondering what I would do, what I would say about all of the conspiratorial happenings around me. Old Mabel, the kindly grandmother who was the most successful street beggar in all of downtown Portland, came up to me, and gave me one of her sweet smiles, before being transformed into an evil witch who cackled and said, *You know what you must do, don't you? Do it! Do it!*

Except I didn't know. I could hear bombs exploding on the distant horizon. A whole platoon of heavily armed soldiers disembarked from the MAX train, and streamed, heads down, arms ready, into Finnegan's Toys. *Why hadn't they called me?* I looked around for my weapon and couldn't find it anywhere. *That's why they hadn't called me! I wasn't ready!* My eyes fell on an AK-47 in the hands of an Iraqi militant who seemed distracted and was looking down at his watch. With reflexes trained over months of readiness exercises, I reached out, grabbed it, and turned it on its original owner. He was caught totally off guard.

"Snake! Snake!" Cole's face blocked my view of the enemy. "Snake! You gotta give that guy back his umbrella!"

I gazed past him toward the now unarmed Iraqi, who appeared, even so, ready to come after me in hand-to-hand combat. "No can do, Cole! My buddies just went in there lookin' for WMDs and I have to go in with 'em. This weapon is my ticket to ride!"

"What weapon? It's not even frickin' rainin'!"

"What are you afraid of, Snake?" This question had come from the Peacemaker. *Funny. I don't remember seeing him in combat before.* Still, his question wormed its way into my brain. *What am I afraid of?*

"Letting down my buddies," I said immediately. Wasn't that obvious? "Being shot at when I can't even see the shooter!" *Hell, a fatal attack can come from anywhere.* "Stepping on something that can blow my legs off." *I can't even feel my legs right now!* "Having to watch myself kill a little child again and again and again . . . " Her eyes had looked at me with the shock of innocence lost before she fell. I found myself on my knees in a pool of blood. *Was it mine or hers? Was it mine or hers? I just have to know! God, let it be mine!*

Gentle arms lifted me to my feet. Cole and the Peacemaker.

"You gotta take your meds again, Snake." For an old shithead, Cole could have such love in his eyes.

"Why?" I asked. "It never goes away. It just lurks in the shadows."

Still, I had no more finished speaking than I felt the little tablet being pushed down my throat.

******

I looked up at a clear blue sky—well, clear except for one little cloud now passing behind the top of one of downtown Portland's taller buildings. I felt a cool breeze on my face.

I looked around and discovered I was lying on a bench near Pioneer Square. Cole and the Peacemaker stood off to the side.

The Peacemaker smiled at me. "There's nothing here to be scared of, Snake. Iraq is all behind you, and we've spread the word you have no money."

"S'right," said Cole. "Now you're just a poor crazy Black dude, and ain't nobody goin' to waste their time trying to roll a poor crazy Black dude."

The Peacemaker's face became more somber. "Hey, if anyone's looking to roll someone, they're going to roll me. I still get some investment money."

Cole quickly looked around. "I wouldn't say that quite so loud if I was you," he said. "That's not exactly something ya want known on the street around here."

“Doesn’t matter,” the Peacemaker said. “Besides, they would also probably rather roll you, Cole. You’ve got his drugs.”

Cole quickly pulled my bottle of meds out of his pocket, and with great fanfare for the crowd of people standing about fifteen feet away, stuffed them into the Peacemaker’s pocket. But I, in turn, reached into his pocket, pulled the bottle out and threw it under an approaching MAX train. The little container bounced up on a rail and was crushed to powder.

“Okay, Snake,” said Cole, “next time your little mind boards a flight to Iraq, I’m outta here!”

I looked into his eyes. “Don’t do that, Cole. I need you.”

The look of shock on Cole’s face made it appear like someone had just shot him in the gut, except there was no gunshot and no blood. “Yeah, that ain’t good. You don’t wanna hear about the people who needed me once. There wouldn’t be a decent positive reference among ‘em. So those words—‘I need you’—that’s like sayin’ put on my blindfold and give me my last cigarette.”

“Hey, I *just* don’t want to have to go over to the mission and eat by myself, that’s all. Don’t get all dramatic on me.”

Cole sat next to me on the bench again, still wide-eyed. “Yeah, well, I’m not going to babysit ya anymore, if that’s what you’re lookin’ for.”

I ignored the comment, sat back on the bench, and began people watching. That’s what I do most of my day, when I’m actually aware of my day. But I have to admit that a fear crept into the back of my mind concerning what I would do without the meds I had just thrown under the MAX train. I could get more but it might take a while.

I'm not sure which of us first felt something strange, but as Cole began checking the faces of the people around us, I realized I was already doing the same, just more anxiously. "Hey, what happened to the Peacemaker?" The words were Cole's.

I went into Iraq mode and more carefully surveyed our surroundings. The crowd which had gathered had now dispersed, and the Peacemaker was nowhere to be found.

Cole stood up to get a better view. "You know, he seemed really concerned about you. Why would he just run off all of the sudden without sayin' anything?"

That didn't seem right to me either. "You know, I don't know if this was just part of the way my crazy little mind works these days, but I remember seeing a white dude in an old, faded blue down jacket, along with an older Black dude over by Peterson's window. They seemed to be watching me. Did you see them in the crowd after you gave me my meds?"

"Yeah, come to think of it. I've been seein' 'em around together the last couple of weeks. None too friendly, though."

Cole and I looked at each other. "Where would he go?"

We both jumped up quickly, and without even conferring on direction ran full speed toward Pioneer Square. I got there first, but the Peacemaker was nowhere to be found. Cole joined me but was too bent over huffing and puffing to help with a visual search. I saw Maria, a woman I knew to be an illegal immigrant. Because of that status, I knew she always kept her eyes open, and so I quickly ran to her.

Yes, she had seen the Peacemaker, with two younger men, one young Anglo and one Black guy like me. Those latter two appeared really angry with him, but he seemed to be trying to smooth things over, to pacify them. They were heading north on Yamhill in the direction of the Willamette River.

No sooner had Cole come up beside me than I bolted in the direction Maria had indicated.

"Hey, hold up!" Cole said. "I gotta rest!"

"No time!" I said. "I'm headin' toward the Burnside Bridge. You come when you can."

I'm not sure what made me know it was the Burnside Bridge. Maria had only said *toward the Willamette,* but something inside of me, something with roots in all of my trauma, was saying that there was danger, and danger for some reason meant the sheltered places under the west end of the Burnside Bridge. On Saturdays the Saturday Market spread out there, but during the week it was a place where shadows gathered.

Just as I couldn't wait for Cole, I also couldn't wait for the streetlights—crossing in the middle of blocks, slithering through traffic. Still, my focus was set, and nothing could slow me down. I made my way down First Avenue and crossed toward the underside of the bridge.

Along the sidewalk people moved with unhurried pace. They paid little regard to anything but their private agendas, as well as the faces and bodies of the more attractive ones who passed them. They weren't paying attention to the shadows.

Had I not been looking for it, perhaps even I would not have seen where the assault occurred. A nonresistant silhouette being thrown violently to the ground. Stomping and kicking motions highlighted by the flashes of light sifted through bridge pillars, beams, and surrounding buildings. Arms raised with rocks in hand.

The assailants didn't see me coming.

I had always excelled in hand-to-hand combat. This was because having someone so close seeking to snuff out my life got my adrenaline flowing. In any case, in two quick movements I had the Black assailant upended and neutralized. He wasn't getting up again soon, I knew. I was unsure of the guy in the faded blue down jacket. The two seemed to have had a skirmish between them, and the younger white guy already lay on the ground, dazed.

I looked down at the Peacemaker and caught my breath. With my body shaking, I got down on my hands and knees and crawled to his side. I lifted his head into my lap and put my shivering hand on his neck where I knew a pulse should be. There was nothing. His chest was as motionless as the concrete on which he lay. Blood trickled down from a deep indentation in his skull. I took my sleeve and gently wiped it from his face.

"Oh, God, you can't do this to us!" I whispered, although I was sure the beaten man could no longer listen. "We need you on the street. What will we do without you?"

I heard a moan behind me and looked to see the young white dude in the faded blue jacket. He had recovered enough to sit up. I was getting ready to hit him when I saw the look in his eyes. I had seen that look only once before when I was briefly stationed in Italy and had gone to the Sistine Chapel. *The Condemned Sinner*. Oh, and I had seen it other times too, now that I think about it. Every time I looked in the mirror in Iraq.

I returned my attention to the fallen Peacemaker. "You were the biggest shithead of us all," I whispered. "You knew this would happen, and you quietly walked right into it. You knew. Why?"

As I looked down at his silent face, I got my answer. It was the face of peace.

Cole tells me that I never had any combat flashbacks after finding the Peacemaker. It makes sense. The Peacemaker's mission had been accomplished. My new one had just begun.

Taking Inventory

People say I don't have anything, but I do. I take inventory every day. I have two shopping carts in which I carry my life. Nobody else I know has more than one.

In my lead cart I have:

One sleeping bag, torn and patched with duct tape

One pillow

One teddy bear

One book without a cover (I want to read it someday)

One old radio like I had when I was a teen (needs a battery)

One nearly new hubcap

One old picture of my mother (taped together—someone tore it!)

Two flashlights (I had three, but someone stole one!)

Three travel brochures (two for Italy, one for Australia)

Three pretty rocks

Five Bibles from the Baptist church (they let you have them for free)

Twenty feet of computer cable.

I push my lead cart ahead of me when I walk. My other cart I pull behind me. In it I have:

One dress with only a few tears

One extra pair of tennis shoes, only slightly too large for my feet

One pair of men's baggy jeans (Although I am a woman, I thought they might fit me

someday)

One partial roll of duct tape

One pink comforter, missing just a little stuffing, patched with duct tape

One old nineteen-inch black and white television set

Four baseball caps, various sizes

Five old magazines: two *Newsweek*, 1997; two *People*, 2002; one *National Geographic,*

2003

Twenty-five feet of leaky garden hose, also patched with duct tape.

They're not interested in what you have in your stupid little carts, Janie!

I take inventory of my life seven or eight times a day: when I get up every morning after sleeping under the Burnside Bridge; when I finish eating or playing the piano at First Baptist Church; right before I go to bed at night; and whenever I see someone suspicious staring at me (okay, maybe more than eight times a day).

They call me Crazy Jane. Yeah, they do. I don't know why. Is it crazy to want to keep people away from your things? Paranoid is the word they use. I say, a little fear is a pretty sane thing, provided you want to stay alive. I watched an old alley cat once. Her eyes always opened wide at every little sound. Make one move toward her and she would slink away quickly, not running in one consistent direction, but darting first to the right and then to the left. Even if you were to get close enough to pet her gently, her eyes would narrow to slits, and she would snarl and hiss and bare teeth that could rip the skin off your hand before you had time to flinch.

She was a smart cat. She was like me.

I told you to stay away from alley cats and stray dogs, you stupid little girl!

"I'm not stupid! I'm not stupid! I'm not stupid!"

Where was I? Oh, yes. Crazy Jane. Some people call me that because I passed up the chance to play piano professionally. Yeah, they say, *she could make money doing that and wouldn't have to live on the street.* Yeah, really. Talk about crazy. Having people breathing down my neck while I play, judging me, comparing me to others, making me play even when the music isn't in me. I know that life. I used to play in competition. Won most of them, too.

You should have won ALL of them—could have, too, if you would have worked harder, like I told you!

I don't want anyone judging me when I play. I just want to play. I say it's crazy to play the piano for any other reason than to feel. Or to fight with a memory. Or to rise above the pain and ugliness. Certainly not to please someone else.

Not me?

"No, Mother!"

My mother used to say—when I couldn't hear her, and there was no danger of my becoming complacent with mistakes, or of my getting a swelled head—that I could play Rachmaninov in a way that would make you think the world was shattering and being reassembled right before your eyes.

That's what I want to do. That's why I want to play.

I do sometimes play for others, but only for people needing to hear, and only for people with gentle voices. Is that being crazy? I'm not crazy. I'm not.

Other people think I'm crazy because I hear voices they don't hear. But, tell me, what is so great about the voices other people hear on the streets of Portland, Oregon? I hear them, too. People preaching on street corners, telling you you're going to hell. (Like I haven't already been *there* before. Been spending my life trying to get out.) People trying to sell you stuff (I have all I need and my carts are full.) People trying to get you to sign a petition or vote for some bozo who says he'll make things better. Yeah, right. I really need to listen to *those* voices.

Listen to your mother, you stupid girl!

One voice I don't mind listening to is that of the Peacemaker. They say he used to be a teacher at Portland State

University, but made some mistakes, and so ended up on the street. People who have made mistakes don't judge you. They know what it's like to fall short of what someone expected of you. He likes my music.

You stay away from those dirty boys!

"He's not a dirty boy, mother!"

You don't know that, you naïve little girl! I have heard stories . . .

I like to play my piano in the fellowship hall of the First Baptist Church. They have a Yamaha Grand piano that sings with the voice of heaven. When I play there, I know in my mind my audience is the audience of heaven, with God's angels leaning over the balcony, whispering to each other words of admiration, fluttering their wings in peace and contentment.

My mother is not among them.

Maybe it is a little crazy to keep hearing your mother's voice five years after she died, when you are yourself over forty years old. But I don't do it because I want to. I do it because it's always there, inside my head. Do normal people have that happen to them? I don't know. I've never known what normal people do.

The Peacemaker has listened to me play several times, certainly more than anyone else I have allowed to listen. The first time I was playing a relatively simple piece, *Für Elise* by Beethoven, perhaps his most popular piano composition. It is music for broken hearts, written by the classical genius to express his agony over being shunned by his one true love for the love of another. I didn't know at first that the Peacemaker was there. So, I was playing only for myself and my audience of angels. My heart has been broken so many times that I imagine it being held together by the same duct tape that patches my comforter, my sleeping bag, and my garden hose. Not that I really had a chance with any man, except in my mind. I was always plain.

One ugly kid, that's for sure. You can't blame me for that, you know.

"Plain Jane." Well, it's better than "Crazy Jane." As a plain girl, my heart was broken the most by relationships that never were. A cute boy who stopped by, in order to be nice to me. A guy who smiled at me in passing. A man my mother knew who did not ignore me. Out of such I could manufacture months of daydreams. Then they would move away, get married, or declare themselves as gay, and *Für Elise* would apply a balm to my soul. I don't think Beethoven ever married. I like to think maybe Beethoven wrote *Für Elise* about a relationship of his that never was, either.

Anyway, as I played *Für Elise* on this occasion, I was, as always, lost in my past. When I finished, I sensed another's presence, and I turned and saw the Peacemaker sitting on the floor, his head between his knees, weeping. My music had done its job.

I think I played for him for an hour on that occasion. During the whole time I played he didn't say a word, and when I had finished, he came up behind me, put his right hand gently on my shoulder, and then walked away.

Oh, my God, you love him, don't you? When will you ever learn?

"Shut up, Mother!"

That wasn't the only time the Peacemaker came by to hear me play. One time he sent a friend, whom I had also met. A friend looking for healing from her memories. It started out really well. She had a story that nobody believed. She had been a body double for Judy Garland in some of her movies and had even danced with Gene Kelly. I played to resurrect her memories, and it worked! "Over the Rainbow." "Get Happy!" I know my angels were watching, and one came down and took hold of her body, and she danced! She danced as if a movie camera had captured her memories and projected them right there onto the floor of the First Baptist Church. Her perfection of movement made me feel that I had to match her with a perfection of musical performance, and with my adrenaline flowing, I was connecting with her note for note, rhythm for rhythm. Still, within my heart there was a rising fear. *What if I missed a note? What if I failed and her beautiful memories all collapsed in a heap around her?* And then it happened. I missed a note. It was there in my head to be played, and I just missed it altogether!

I tried not to panic, but my heart began to race, and my hands felt heavy. It was hard to breathe.

You missed the note!

"I missed the note!"

You call yourself a piano player, you incompetent child!

"I missed the note! I should never have tried that piece!"

I looked down at my hands, and they had stopped playing.

You thought you could do this without me, didn't you? You thought you could play without listening to me! Well, now look at what happened!

"I did well until that moment. I did!"

You had your pathetic little audience, and you were trying to impress them! You were playing for them, and not me!

I looked around—the Peacemaker and the Judy Garland lady were no longer there.

You will never play well again, because you won't listen to ME!

I got up so quickly the piano bench turned over and I fell flat on my back. An image flashed in my mind of when I was little, and I had knocked the fishbowl over, and our goldfish had just thrashed about on the floor, except now I was the fish, flailing about, fighting for air.

Ha! Look at you! Scared of me? Well, you should be!

The voice actually helped me get moving. I got to my feet and ran quickly to the back door, where I had stashed my carts. Opening that door and pulling out two carts was a challenge in normal circumstances, but now that I was feeling pursued, it was a nearly impossible task. And I kept hearing her voice, laughing! By the time I finally did get my second cart through the door, fear was coming at me from every direction, and I put all cautions aside. That's when the back cart tipped and fell, dumping its precious contents. Startled, I tripped and fell, sending the front cart rolling toward the street, where it also tipped over, spilling the remainder of my life into the gutter. The laughter coming from my mind reverberated in that narrow alley where the church stored its garbage for collection.

And then I saw them there, picking it all up. The Peacemaker and Judy Garland's body double had come back, and they calmly walked over to the cart by the street, returned it to an upright position, and began carefully replacing its contents. Understand, I never let *anyone* touch my things! But I did this time. It was like a gentle, skillful surgical team was repairing my insides after a traumatic collision. The hand of God had touched me, not to remove a rib, but to restore one. It is not good for the woman to be alone.

I got up quickly and searched for my things to get them back in my other cart. It wasn't easy, as some items had fallen behind or under trash containers. What really bothered me was after I had picked up all I could find, I wanted to look over at my two friends, to give them a smile, to thank them, to let them know that what they had done had touched me. I couldn't. I couldn't because my mind became so overwhelmingly absorbed in whether I had lost anything. I had to take inventory. I had to!

I began with the lead cart:

One sleeping bag, torn and patched with duct tape

One pillow

One teddy bear, not in its right place

One book without a cover, now even more ripped and torn

One old radio like I had when I was a teen, not in its right place

One old picture of my mother, now more bent and wrinkled

One flashlight

One travel brochure, Italy

Two pretty rocks

Five Bibles from the Baptist church, none in the right place

Twenty feet of computer cable.

I looked around for the missing items. I know the Peacemaker and the Judy Garland lady were nearby then, but I couldn't pay attention to them while all was in disarray. I had to make sure everything was fixed first, didn't I? The rock was easiest to find, right there in the gutter, as if it belonged with other less distinctive rocks. The other flashlight had rolled down to the corner. The other travel brochures had blown into some nearby bushes, and the hub cap had rolled across the street. A couple of cars honked at me when I went across the street to get it, but I didn't care. When I got back to the cart, I made sure everything in the cart was in its right place, and then I turned my attention to my second cart:

One dress with only a few tears, a little more soiled

One extra pair of tennis shoes

One pair of men's baggy jeans

One pink comforter, missing just a little stuffing

One old black and white television set, the screen now cracked

Four baseball caps, various sizes

Five old magazines, all soiled: two *Newsweek*, 1997; two *People*, 2002; one *National*

Geographic, 2003

Twenty-five feet of leaky garden hose.

I found my precious duct tape, where it had rolled behind a garbage bin. Of course, everything else was in its proper place, because I had repacked it myself. Now I could thank the Peacemaker and the Judy Garland lady. I looked around for them, but they were gone. They hadn't just rolled away. They were gone.

******

For days without end, my life was out of kilter—in spite of the fact that all my inventory was back in place. I counted it more frequently, to make sure. My mother laughed. However many days passed, I finally once again encountered the old woman who claimed to have served as Judy Garland's stand-in and occasional body double. She was talking to the Snake, down at Pioneer Square. They were sitting on a bench toward the top of that sunken plaza in central downtown Portland. I walked up to her with my carts and waited until she looked up at me.

"Thank you," I said.

She scrunched up her face and tilted her head. "For what?"

"For when you and the Peacemaker helped me pick up my things. You both left before I could thank you. I haven't seen the Peacemaker yet."

A tear came to her eye, and she looked down at the sidewalk.

"What?"

Her gaze returned to me. "The Peacemaker was mugged last night," she said quietly. "I'm afraid he is dead."

I'm not sure what I did at first. I remember just staring at her for a while. Mother was laughing. I remember, too, the old woman got up from where she was sitting and gave me a hug. I let her, but I didn't hug back. I turned and left, pushing and pulling my two carts. Every time I came to a side street, I turned to the right or to the left, with no reason. After what seemed like hours of doing that, I wasn't sure where I was, and I knew I didn't know where I was going. I just wanted to escape the threat. I wanted to be where I was not.

At some point I made it down to the spot underneath the Burnside Bridge where they say he died. A couple of police officers were still there, finishing their investigation. One was removing the yellow tape they put up for such investigations. I had been there many times to sleep at night, and yet the place seemed more cold and more lonely, even though it was still summer and the officers were there. I shivered and wrapped myself in my own arms.

Just as I was turning to leave, I spied a rock about the size of a baseball a few feet away from where the officers were finishing their work. It was plain, with no distinctive colors or features, such as the three rocks in my cart. But I noticed one little feature it had that the others did not. A reddish black spot of blood. I knew the officers might want it, but they had had their chance. I picked it up, put it in my lead cart, and left.

I walked for about a half hour before I finally stopped and looked at my new rock again. It seemed more beautiful than I had initially thought. I carefully put it in a spot in the cart where it was less likely to rub against anything else. I had to keep it safe. Then I found the item it would replace on my inventory. I picked up the torn picture of my mother and looked at it briefly for one last time. Then I tore it again and tossed it in a nearby trash container.

I had found a new voice.

At the Barricade

A war is being waged on the streets of America. The true battleground for this conflagration is not the back alleys, the shadowy dead-end urban streets, or the bridge culverts, as strewn as they are with wounded; but the human hearts of all who shuffle, stride, and dodge their way along those engineered avenues. The war wages on within each soul—between the divine and the satanic in the human heart—and the missiles that hit one another are always the collateral damage of attempted self-destruction.

The world explodes from friendly fire.

I once pretended I was just an observer in these battles, looking out from my university window, as if from a castle turret, ready to objectively describe it all. *Professor of English Literature.* Talking about other people who were also writing about other people who were living life. Then Life reached up and grabbed me by the nape of the neck, like a bitch shaking her inattentive pup, and then throwing me into the fray. No more simply observing now.

Shoulder to shoulder with others, I stand in this furtive war.

I do see and participate in victories, and people win them under the banner of hope. Victories won over the dark side of battered psyche. Victories won over ancient trauma as well as yesterday's fall. Victories won when, in a skirmish with fear, a timid soul turns and faces the battle.

They call me the Peacemaker and I have been deployed in this battle as it's fought among the homeless in Portland, Oregon. I earned the title through my status as one of the walking wounded. The healing I seek is the healing I share with others. The hope that lures me forward is the hope I unveil before Portland's other fallen.

******

It was while walking down by Pioneer Square that I saw the young man. I sensed I had seen him before, but not until he turned and recognized me with a smile, did I realize the connection. By then I had hesitated too long to run.

"Hey, Professor!"

Having no white flag to wave, I submitted to my fate and smiled back. "Hello, Mike!"

He walked over, carrying his lunch, and sat down next to me. I joined him sitting on the stairs. As I had suspected, he wanted to talk about old times. Good old days to him. The more I asked him about his life today, the more he would shift from his present successes (and with a job at Nike, he had many) to where he saw it all beginning—my classes at Portland State University. We spoke about books and discussions of long ago. Then he rose to go. He picked up his trash together with the crumbs of the Greek gyro he had been eating. One more question came to his lips.

"Do you ever wish you had stayed?"

I had not noticed before, but some questions really don't come from a person's mouth, no matter what evidence one might enlist to the contrary. Some questions just rise out of the dust of the earth and are created by the Lord of the Universe while you stand there, waiting. This one arose as one of those questions.

"Come on, Teach! You fielded a lot more difficult questions than that all of the time at Portland State. Do you ever wish you had stayed?"

I looked into the young man's eyes. He had no idea he had backed me into a minefield. He would not have acted so maliciously.

I remembered him sitting in the second row of seats in the Freshman English class I had taught six years ago. Mike Ross' eyes were focused now, whereas then they seemed to bounce around the classroom, from the ample cleavage of a coed, to an outside window, and back to me as I delved into the philosophical and theological issues embedded in Melville's *Moby Dick.* At that point in time, before my self-destruction, teaching young people like him, helping them to free themselves from the bonds of distraction and triviality, had been one of my life's greatest pleasures.

"Staying where I used to be was never a choice I was offered," I said.

I stood and tried to leave, but he took hold of my arm. "I hated that you had to leave. You were absolutely my favorite prof—no contest."

I smiled at first, partially because of his enthusiasm for what once was. Then as I looked into his eyes, he began to remind me of another young man, one far less accepting and at the same time even more important to my life. My son had once idolized me, but now I couldn't even get him to speak to me. I had seen him not too long before, wearing an old faded blue jacket, with a hole in one elbow. He had seemed to be running in a pretty rough crowd. Word on the street was he had been selling drugs, and when business turned bad, mugging the occasional street person. But he no longer saw me as his father.

I now found myself running.

By the time my legs burned too much to move them forward any longer, I had made my way to Washington Park, with its beautiful gardens and its view overlooking the city of Portland. I sat down on a bench and leaned back, seeking to catch my breath. I just wanted to look down at the grayness of the cloudy sky and buildings of concrete and steel. I most certainly did not want at that moment in time to see the faces of people. I do like people. I like them immensely, especially the female ones. However, in relationship to those same female persons my life had failed miserably.

So, of course, because I wanted to get away from people, people came to me; they sought me out—not to talk to, not to consult or to even notice at all—but to stroll past and ignore. Three older high school girls bounced down the paved walkway, spinning around as they walked, periodically coming together to share their little confidences, and then caroming off each other afterward in fits of laughter. Their mouths all moved at the same time, as if they were divulging the various thoughts of one mind. They rolled their eyes, a coquettish gesture they seemed to have practiced together all their lives; and they used the words "like" and "totally" in virtually every sentence, at least those I could hear.

And, of course, all three girls were pretty. God would not send anyone to ignore me if they were less than beautiful.

No sooner had these girls gone than a young couple followed close behind. I had to take a close look at the angular young man to be sure he was not a hologram of my own self at that age—a hologram projected from within my memory out onto this new era, this era from which I so often felt disconnected. The girl with whom he walked could easily have been Emily at that age. Emily—before our marriage, before having my vigorous, formerly bright-eyed and talented young son, before her face was crushed in anguish by my inability to be faithful. The young man leaned close to kiss her and at the same time brushed his hand against the visible softness of her shapely, spandex-covered bottom.

I saw the young brunette's tongue flick out from between her lips as they kissed, and I saw the bulge behind his jeans' zipper. And they moved on. I'm sure they never even saw me.

I have had a lot of time to think about hell of late, to think about whether such a place or state exists, and what it might be like. Jean-Paul Sartre had a character in his play *No Exit* say, "Hell is other people." For me, I would say: *hell is that hole left in your heart when you hunger for people you have driven away.* It can be an eternal hole in which burns an eternal fire, or it can be a vacuum which sucks all of life around you into its blackness.

I report how the war goes from the perspective of this lone combatant. And, as you see, I am not winning. There are times when I tremble at the edge of the abyss.

So, on this occasion I descended from the hill Washington Park occupied to return to the urban valley and see if I could once again touch heaven. I found myself in the food line at the Baptist church.

The food line at this particular church is a main gathering spot for my new family, Portland's downtown poor and homeless. Some there had surrendered sanity in order to adjust to a world that often does not make sense. Crazy Jane stood in line with her shopping cart overflowing with possessions others had left in some dumpster. She would have the normal discussion with the volunteers at the door as to why she must leave that cart outside under their watch and care. She would only give in when the aromas within the building overpowered the fears within her scarred memory.

Some came because it was the only locale in their world where they did not feel out-of-place. Ruth Anne now entered the door. Born a man, but discovering she was far too gentle for that sex, she let the doctors transform her into the work God probably had in mind from the beginning. The Snake, a veteran of a war he could not leave behind in Iraq, belonged here as well, as did other vets, some of whom still wore their hiding clothes—their military fatigues—to a place where they did not need to hide.

No wonder I felt like I belonged here, more than I had ever felt I belonged in academia.

"Hey, Peacemaker!"

The greeting from Cole soothed me.

"Hey, Cole!"

I find peace in going where everybody knows my name.

******

The best churches are true sanctuaries, not just places for the privileged to come and thank God for their privilege, but holy places where the battered and worn can come to find safety—if only for a few brief moments. What I like best about going to this particular church for a meal are the eyes which look at you and smile. When you are homeless, people walking along the street look the other way. You become a streetlamp that one watches out of the corner of their eye, so as not to walk into it. But here you can be a person again, if for just a little while.

"Good afternoon, Peacemaker," said Nancy, an older Asian woman who never hesitated to greet me, even out on the street. "I've got some stir-fry here I put together myself. How about it?"

"Pile it on, Nancy. You know I can't resist your stir-fry."

Further on down the line, an attractive teenage girl, whose name I did not know, served me a pretty smile and offered me dessert. It brought a tear to my eye. She probably thought it was the food.

Looking at all the lonely souls gathered in that place, I put in perspective the latest salvos in my war. When I had fled, I had sought escape from my own falling, from my own past. What I returned to was others, and a chance to lift them to a higher plane. In helping them find their peace, I knew I would find my own.

While focusing on the hurting of others in that hall, I saw him again—not my student, but another young man. Same old faded blue down jacket, with the hole in the elbow. A cold, bitter look on his face. He came through the food line with an older Black guy who looked mad at the world. Had I been fully healed I would have stayed. Perhaps I would have casually walked over and asked to be introduced to his friend. I would have felt their wounds—not with my hands but with my heart. But my own wounds seem to know when they are in danger, and they withdrew deep within me.

I left without even talking to the son who had not spoken to me in over a year.

I went first to Pioneer Square but found no respite. Everyone seemed to be running. At first, I thought they ran *toward,* but then after some reflection, all seemed to be running *away from.* I knew what I ran away from, but the thought that others were also seeking such escape got me wondering what they ran away from. Maybe the rejection and judgments of parents, judgments they thought just might be true. Maybe they ran away from shadows, uncertainties, things that jump up and frighten them in the night of one's childhood and continue to emerge from the darknesses of adulthood. Maybe they ran from themselves, their failures of heart, their failures of soul. I felt all of that.

I started wandering wherever my heart led me, and my heart has never led me toward running away. I spent that night talking to other homeless people under the Burnside Bridge.

The Snake sat there with us. The good news was that he knew he was there. Quite often his mind fled back to Iraq, the country he could find no way to leave. Crazy Jane rocked back and forth in her own little world. The good news for her was she sat with real people. Even with their neuroses they were far less frightening than the specters of her mind. Cole sat beside the Snake next to our little fire. In the coldness of his nights, he had driven away everyone except for this little group around the fire. Still, something compelled him to try to drive away even these. He laughed at a sacred memory of an old woman.

"I believe her." Simple words, but the moment I said them, I saw her old, wrinkled face lift, even in the flickering flames of our little street fire. I had spoken without thinking, and yet after speaking those magic words I realized I did in fact believe her memory of being Judy Garland's stand-in. My belief found support in only a few bits of circumstantial evidence: she was about the age Judy Garland would have been had she lived; she stood about five feet tall, the approximate height of that cultural icon; and even as an old woman she had the wide-eyed look of innocence. Belief filters such little details with a healing generosity, and I saw an old woman who had explored the land of rainbows.

I never knew the woman's given name, but I knew her battle. She fought her war against insignificance and the pain of feeling her contribution to life remained unacknowledged. Her greatest moment had occurred when she lived in the shadow of a star, and people didn't even believe that. Now she roamed the streets, ignored by people who thought they had better things to do than listen to her. So, I listened.

The next day we went our separate ways, but I knew where I might find her that afternoon. I had suggested she listen to Crazy Jane play the piano in the reception hall of the Baptist church at a time when no one else would be around. I knew she would be impressed. What surprised me at least a little was that once Crazy

Jane knew the woman listened, she started playing songs from Judy Garland movies. And this woman danced! Ninety years old and she danced as if she had been transported to a world where age didn't matter, and the rhythm of an ancient spirit could flow unimpeded by arthritic joints and muscles functioning with a time delay. She danced and flowed, and when she finished, I applauded. I applauded and we smiled a shared smile.

******

Thinking of victories in the war lightens my spirit. Perhaps this is how it feels for those recounting stories of the Battle of the Bulge, Iwo Jima, or Hamburger Hill.

Of course, less-than-victorious moments also come to mind. There are times when I have to retreat from a near massacre. Such was the case when, for some inexplicable reason, I went back to Portland State University the day the old woman danced.

Why did I go? Perhaps my pain drew me there. As an adolescent I had been drawn to horror movies—movies about every possible fear, movies that should have driven me to hiding, but instead drew me to come of my own volition, surrendering the security of my parents' suburban comfort for moments of abject terror. Arms, legs, and even heads—severed. Footsteps following behind—not just innocently creaking floorboards, but creatures encountered only in my nightmares. Evil eyes staring from the shadows of every room, and behind the glare of every window. Maybe we are drawn by the myth that fear can be left in the chosen theater of a moment.

Of course, to the neutral observer, Portland State University did not come across as a horror movie. Whatever terror students felt about coming tests or teacher judgments or what doors to their dreams might slam shut on that day, they walked the streets and sidewalks mostly with alacrity. For some, life rather seemed all a romantic comedy, with just enough tension to assure happy tears when it all came together in the end. For some, it evolved as a mystery, where one could be confident that the hero would solve all the puzzles. In the end, it would be elementary.

Or maybe life flashed by as an action movie gone bad. From where I stood, I could almost see the office where it had all blown up.

"Couldn't help returning to the scene of the crime, huh?"

I turned around, and my stomach instantly tied up in a knot. There stood the young man in the old, faded blue down jacket. Next to him a taller, older Black man leaned against a streetlight, his arms folded, with a cold and steely glare in his eyes. They impressed upon me as the eyes of a hit man awaiting his orders.

"I think of this place as the scene of a whole former life," I said. "My triumphs, as well as my crimes." I sought to release my visage from the tension which had grabbed hold of me, and at the same time set free the tender feelings buried inside me for the young man I once read stories to at night. I smiled. "How are you doing, son?"

My words and expressions, meant to soothe, seemed to hit him with a jolt. He pulled back and looked over at his companion.

"Son? He must be talking about you, Willie. With all the other women he screwed while pretending to be teaching them, I'm sure at least one of them must have been Black. Who knows? Maybe you are his son!"

"I know you're angry, and you have a right to be," I said. "But my mistakes don't change our relationship." Then before I gave a thought to evaluating appropriateness, my twisted humor stepped in, and I did my best impression of James Earl Jones' classic voice role. "Derek, I am your father."

"Ah, good. Darth Vader! A different kind of heavy breathing for you, I've gotta say, but still—the Prince of Darkness. Appropriate. Appropriate."

"I said I'm sorry a thousand times. What else can I say, Derek? What else can I do?"

"Oh, you're doing enough," my son said, pausing for effect. "You're out here on these stinkin' streets, suffering in the cold and rain, and I've got to tell ya—I love every minute of it! I love it every time I see you out here, thinking about what you once had, and what you threw away, all because you couldn't resist getting inside some coed's panties. I absolutely love it."

I nodded. "How's your mother?"

Derek motioned toward his friend. "This is who I'm hangin' with now. Does he look like my mother? Last I saw her, she was givin' it away to any guy who wanted it. Damaged goods, ya know. A Walmart special. I couldn't stand watchin' anymore."

And so it went, with me unfurling a white flag while he loaded another round. Each volley tore through my flesh to uncover my bloody soul.

"You're right," I said. "I belong here."

Derek cocked his head and squinted his eyes at me. "What?"

"I said, 'You're right.' You don't have to do anything more to convince me."

Turning and walking away from your flesh and blood, from one you nurtured as a child and whom you still love, is as hard of a thing as a person can do, but I did it. I did it because I knew there was no life for either of us in the past. Still, my son saw our past with too much bitterness to let go of it.

"You aren't done with me, old man!" he yelled for the world to hear.

I gave him a parting wave. "Do what you need to do, son."

******

I thought I had escaped my encounter with my son without permanent injury, but as I walked around, I felt more like I was floating. I couldn't feel my feet or my hands. What I sought to shut out of my mind throbbed within my body. So, when I found myself near the Congregational church, it seemed natural to open the door and go into their sanctuary.

I knew, of course, that this church left the door to its sanctuary open during the day so it could be a true sanctuary. In Church tradition, and sometimes in legal tradition, you could flee to a sanctuary if you were pursued by some danger; whether an angry enemy, officers of the law, or opposing combatants in a war. You could find respite for your soul, as well as your body.

I staggered through the door of this worship center, down the center aisle to the front pew, where I sat down. I was alone. For what must have been five or ten minutes I stared at the floor and breathed. Then I looked up at the cross. My heart could see blood, even though my mind recognized this as a production of my spirit. My heart could see loving eyes, even though no actual figure hung there. I found myself collapsing face down on the floor. And I cried. I cried all the tears I had dammed up since my fall, all the tears I had hidden under the façade of emotional control which I showed the world. I laid it all down as my offering before my Lord, and he accepted it.

******

The next time I was in Pioneer Square I felt an urgent need to find him—no, not Derek, the student, the student who had asked me that question.

"Do you ever wish you had stayed?"

Yeah, that was the question.

I had to stake out the area for three days, but he did eventually show up. I walked right up to him.

"The answer to your question is 'no.'"

"My question?"

"The last time I saw you here, you asked a question. 'Do you ever wish you had stayed?' The answer to the question is 'no.'"

"Really?"

"Really. In a war like this you don't retreat. Not when your buddies need you."

He looked confused.

"Look," I continued, "I loved teaching young people like you. But I messed up. There's no sugarcoating or excusing that. Still, it was all for naught if I didn't learn from it and pass along something I learned to others—people on the street who had also fallen."

As I looked into Mike Ross' eyes, I could see he was still having trouble processing it all. "Hey, I know several of the girls in my class were really hot," he said. "I can see where—"

"Doesn't matter. Wrong is wrong."

"But they chose to—"

"Doesn't matter."

My former student toyed with what remained of his falafel. Then he looked up into my eyes and smiled. "Yeah, well, you were still the best teacher I ever had. I hate to see that wasted."

"Thanks, but it's not. There's a lot to learn, and a lot to teach out here on the streets."

I could feel the adrenaline surging through my body in a way it hadn't done since those college teaching days.

"You taught me so much."

"Really?" I asked. "Then how about a test? You studied literature under me. Which of the books we read in class would you advise me to re-read, given my present life situation?"

As with any good student, the question was an immediate stimulant to what had become his laconic spirit. He jumped up from the bench and began pacing.

"Yes! That's just the kind of question you would have asked!" He paused and looked up at one of the taller buildings nearby. I could tell he was lost in an eternity of thought. When he quietly strode back to where I stood, he had a smile on his face. "What first came to my mind was *The Catcher in the Rye*, because Holden Caulfield, you know, wanted so much to protect young people from . . . I guess what you would call 'the evils of adulthood.' I always felt like you wanted to do that with your students."

"That's true, the evils I was myself involved in."

"But then I thought, no, that's what you were then. Now your struggle has been with your own behavior, and maybe finding a way to forgive yourself, so I thought *Les Misérables,* the classic story of finding redemption by caring for other people struggling on the street. So, yeah, I think maybe *Les Misérables.*"

I sat down on the bench and slowly nodded, before looking again at my former student. "Okay, you get an 'A.' Sorry I can't put it on a transcript."

He smiled. "Not necessary. I got all I needed from you already." He held out his right hand, and I stood and shook it. "Good luck with your new class," he said. Then he left.

I never saw Mike Ross again, but he had given me courage. Courage to face myself. Courage to be human. And courage to face my pursuing Javert.

My Father's Son

The room was small, intentionally small I thought. They wanted me to feel like everything was closing in on me. They wanted all the accusations they threw at me, as well as the accusations I threw at myself, to build up in that little room like the staleness of the air.

It was okay. I deserved it.

Still, I must tell my story as accurately as I knew how, shining whatever light could be found into the darkness of my own soul. Perhaps talking it all out to police officers would help me do that.

"I didn't kill him. That much I know!"

The two officers glanced at each other, then looked back at me. The one officer seemed pissed, like it offended him to even have to listen to me. But the other one cocked his head to the side and looked at me so intensely that it seemed his gaze would bore into my brain. "Go on!" he said.

Yeah, Go on. How can I "go on" after all that's happened? Okay, I'll try.

*****

Growing up, I was so proud of my father. The man who taught me to read, to hit a baseball, to make camp in the wilderness; that man also taught hundreds, even thousands, who idolized him almost as much as I did. He taught them about books that great teachers have taught through the centuries. He taught them to think and to reach for the stars. They came by at all hours to ask him questions about those books and about life, to tell him about their marriages and their jobs, to seek his advice, as if he were a guru on a mountaintop. Upon leaving they would always look at me like, *what a lucky kid to have such a father.*

I knew boys who hated their fathers, but I had never shared that feeling. Their fathers always left. Left them stinging from a belt wielded as a weapon. Left them to fend against the world on their own. Left them crying their tears against a windowpane rather than coming to visit as promised. My father would never leave.

So, the day my dad left, I knew it must have been my mother's fault. "What did you do to him?" I had said.

Did you ever notice how sometimes when you ask a question when you're really pissed, you don't want an answer? You sure as hell don't want them to tell you the truth. My mom told me the truth, and I didn't believe her. I yelled through my tears, and I threw things at her, things that could have done real damage had they found their mark—a heavy hardbound copy of *Les Misérables* that Dad had given me, an aluminum bat, an old broken printer which had been sitting unused in my room for months. That last one grazed her shoulder, but still she never threw anything back. She just stood there and cried.

When he came back to visit me the first time, he admitted it all. He had been unfaithful to my mother, not just on one occasion, but many. He had been with several of his female students, students he was supposed to be teaching. He was sorry. He had been weak. *But how could he?*

Dad had been my teacher, too. We read *Shane* together, and he used it to teach me about being a real man. Shane was attracted to Joe's wife, Marian, but he resisted because he was a real man. He taught me stories of Christian monks who went their whole lives depriving themselves of sex, because of their religious devotion. We went to church and talked about King David, and how his affair with Bathsheba nearly ruined his kingdom. *Did he ever really believe what he told me?*

When it finally got through to my foggy brain what he had done, what I threw at him I knew had far more potential for damage than what I had thrown at my mother. I threw my most vile words. I told him to never come back. I never wanted to see him again.

When he left, he left me with my rage, and that rage was what would never leave. It startled me awake in the middle of the night, my heart pounding, my eyes darting around the darkened corners of my room, my breath heaving, seeking to suck in the spirit of well-being that had deserted me. My rage rose up early with me and was still going strong when I pulled back the covers of my bed at night. It flared at my mother's instructions. It waxed hot whenever someone else asked me to attend to their emotional needs, their meaningless priorities. It even shot through my heart when a pretty girl looked at me and smiled, smiled as if she thought I was like my father.

I started hanging with Willie because he shared my rage. Willie had always known his father was worthless. His father had left when he was four, and the jerk only came back when he thought he could get some money out of Willie's mom, or when he needed someone to beat on for a while. Willie never knew a man who was there for him. Whatever happened in his life that was good, he made happen with no help from anyone. That was fine for him. That's what he said, anyway. I wanted to be like Willie now.

I didn't want to just forget about Mom, but it was so hard looking at her anymore. What Dad had done just cut her to the core. I looked at this white nightgown she wore, as it lay empty and wrinkled on her bed, and I thought, *God, that's her dead spirit lying there!* So white and pure, but now so empty. Every night it seemed she looked for another guy to fill it, but every morning, *still empty*! So, I couldn't stand it, and I had to leave.

The streets of Portland, Oregon, are a good place for two young dudes just wanting to watch each other's back, and to beat the hell out of the rest of the world. Such a laid-back city. It's not ready for mad-at-the-world.

We spent our days scouting the downtown areas, our nights sleeping under the Burnside or Morrison Street Bridge, and the early hours of morning trolling for targets. There were a lot of drunks around, and we learned which ones had something to be taken. Occasionally, we would adjust our routine to hit someone looking for their car after a late-night theater performance, but that made too much news. People would go out looking for us. Drunks were safer, because nobody cared.

Of course, Willie and I weren't too proud to take advantage of the freebies—meals over at the Baptist church, the Sisters of the Road Café, or the Union Gospel Mission. When the weather got too bad, we would sometimes stay at the mission. That was okay, as long as you attended their services and knew the right words to say. *I'm a terrible, terrible sinner, but Jesus saved me! Praise the Lord! And you got any more o' those pancakes this mornin'?*

I liked it better out on the streets, where you didn't have to go through that crap. Especially where you didn't have to think about sin and guilt. When you're out on the streets at night, the darkness hides a lot, sometimes even from yourself. Yeah, I still had a conscience. But it was like I was mad at it, too. I just stuffed it down into the darkness of my soul. The drugs helped me do that.

Of course, right from the start I knew he was out there, too. My dad. They called him the Peacemaker, which I couldn't figure because I had so little peace, and it was mostly because of him. Willie right away thought we should take him down. We had the opportunities. He always ate at the Baptist church. He only occasionally had anyone with him when he left. He often slept under the Burnside Bridge and slept alone. While people often came to him for advice, the only ones who were around him often were a crazy Iraq veteran called the Snake, and his derelict sidekick Cole, who was known to have a fondness for cheap booze. The Iraq veteran could fight, but he had PTSD and was often off in his own little world. If we kept an eye on him, we could take the Peacemaker while his protection was off trippin' in Iraq. Still, I hesitated to sign off on a plan. I told myself it was because I wanted to be careful. But there was more to it than that. A battle was going on inside of me that I could not understand.

So, here's how it all came down. I told you about the rage, right? If you've never had it eat away at you, then you won't understand. I kept seeing happy families together. Down at Pioneer Square. Going into the shopping mall. Going into one of the downtown churches on Sunday morning. I told Willie we should hang out around Portland State, because there weren't many families strolling through the streets there. But that's when we saw *him.* You would have thought he would have avoided the place where he had fallen, but no. Willie said maybe he was trolling for some tight coed ass—hooked again on his drug, hooked again on what had torn apart the home in which I was raised, hooked again on what had turned my mother into the defeated, quivering mass of flesh I left crying in her room. I was feeling that.

So, I tore into him with my words. He said he was there to reminisce, to remember, and to learn from his failure. He said he was sorry—sorry for what he had done to my mom, to me. He spoke of trying to make up for it all by helping others on the street. When he said these things, the battle inside of me raged all the more. You've got to believe that part of me wanted to believe him, to love him again, and somehow magically go back to having my father again. But part of me was just scared! It's scary to hope you might regain something precious that you have lost. At that moment, the scared part of me won the battle. I told him he was no longer my father. No longer. Nevermore!

I saw him wince. Then he left.

As he walked away, I told him I would laugh as he took his last breath, and that I would piss on his grave. Yeah, I said that. My words now echo in my mind over and over and over again.

******

I'm sorry, I must have blanked out. What was I saying? Oh, yes, what I said to my father. But, you've got to understand that I really didn't laugh when he took his last breath, and I would never do anything to desecrate his grave. You get that, right?

Go on.

That encounter threw me into turmoil. Willie kept egging me on, and maybe if he hadn't . . . I don't know, I can't blame it all on him, but things might have happened differently.

We later went to check out what was happening with Cole and the Snake, to see if they were providing protection. We didn't have to follow them around long, before we witnessed the Snake having his hallucinations about being back in Iraq. Well, he wasn't hallucinating at first, but he was looking really down. Cole was taking care of him like he was the man's nurse or something and my dad . . . the Peacemaker . . . was there, too. He was talking to them about life, and they really listened, like they were in his own personal classroom. In that moment I was kind of proud of him. People really looked up to him. But it also made me angry. He was acting like he never fell, like he was still a real teacher, and he didn't have anything to pay for. The conflict inside of me was tearing me apart! Part of me felt like going over right then and unleashing all of my rage on him in front of the whole world. Part of me just wanted him to hug me.

The Snake noticed us standing there, and we had to look away, like we really weren't watching them at all. It wasn't long, though, before there was a big commotion in their direction, and that's when we noticed the Snake was hallucinating again. He had grabbed some guy's umbrella, and seemed to think it was some kind of semi-automatic rifle. Really weird. Scarily weird. Cole and the Peacemaker were trying to calm him down and get him his meds, and before I realized it, he was looking our way. No, not the Snake, but even scarier. The Peacemaker.

Cole and the Snake didn't seem to notice when he broke away from them and walked our way. I knew I was coming to a moment of decision.

I remember the way his voice was—gentle, calm, and without a trace of fear, How could he have not been afraid? Surely, he remembered my threats! He had to see the anger and hate in Willie's eyes, didn't he? It was as if he had become immunized against the hate and fear that dominated the world Willie and I—and everyone else I knew—had been living in.

The Peacemaker looked into my eyes and smiled. "So, how are you doing now, Son?"

The tears rolled down my eyes. I looked past those tears into the eyes of my father. It hurt so bad! He said nothing more, but I saw the love in those eyes—love I had refused to listen to with my ears. I saw the man who had carried me to bed at night, the man who had taught me to throw a baseball, the man who had soothed my fears during a hundred frightening nights. In spite of my every effort, the Peacemaker had become my dad again.

Still, *how was I doing?* My mouth could not find the words.

I had thought Willie would have seen my transition, and for a moment he seemed to.

"We need a place more private," he said. "Let's go underneath the Burnside Bridge and work this whole thing out."

Did I see his intent? At that moment I was struggling to see anything clearly. But Willie was my friend. He had been with me in the toughest moments of my life. He had slept beside me on asphalt and concrete as the frigid rain of Portland swept over us. When he found food, he shared it with me. Every feeling that emerged from the depths of his own soul, he shared with me, with no hesitation. How could I not trust his direction? Could my father see his intent more clearly? Maybe or maybe not. Maybe he was just surrendering himself into my arms.

As we walked briskly in the direction of our destination, my heart raced, more so than it should have even at that pace. I see now my heart was warning me against barriers that should never be crossed.

Before I realized it, we were there, partially hidden from those in the streets by shadows.

I turned toward my father to look in his eyes again, to see that love again, the love which had so recently brought light to my darkness. But what I saw was the blood! Blood was splattered all over the concrete! Blood streamed down my father's face! Willie hit him over and over again with a large rock in his fist. My father did nothing to defend himself! He said nothing. He just looked at me with those eyes! I grabbed Willie's arm with all my might, but Willie's arm, powered by an anger which had built over a lifetime, easily flung me away. I passed out.

When I came to, I awoke to a nightmare. The Snake came and busted Willie up like a martial arts master disposing of a pissed off drunk. He then shifted a steely gaze toward me, daring me to be next. But then I'm sure he saw. His eyes softened and his warrior form relaxed. He saw the terror in my eyes, eyes which gazed in horror at my father's lifeless form, sprawled out over rock and concrete. Then, as I diverted my eyes to my own self, what I saw was even more crushing to my spirit. My father's blood covered me.

The next thing I remember, I was standing in the Skidmore Fountain, fully clothed, trying to wash away it all.

All night I ran. I'm not sure there is a place in downtown Portland I did *not* run to. I ran to Pioneer Square—why I do not know, other than I was used to being there. I ran to the Union Gospel Mission, even though the doors were closed for the night. I ran to the Baptist church, now dark and gated. I ran to Portland State University, to the spot where I had so recently argued with my father. He was not there. That's when I realized who I was running from in all of my running. I was running from me.

Finally, with more resolve and direction, I ran to the apartment in which my mother now lived. She awoke and buzzed me in.

I almost didn't recognize her as my mother at first, not because she had only recently crawled out of bed, still sleepy, but because of the changed attitude expressed in her face. Gone was the permanent frown. Gone was the furrowed brow. Back was a light in her eyes which I remembered from before the fall.

I was also relieved that there was no man in the apartment, and that I saw none of the empty wine and beer bottles formerly strewn across the living room. Still, I was all the more frightened that this might change because of what had happened, because of what I had done. I felt unimaginably fearful about telling her anything of the night's events. The only thing I feared more was having her be told by someone else.

Of course, after her initial joy at seeing me, she saw the blood. I couldn't wash it *all* out in the Skidmore Fountain. When she saw it, she assumed I had been hurt somehow. The maternal instincts in her kicked in, and she began fussing over me. Talking about getting me to the emergency room and pointing out how much weight I had lost and how pale I looked. I was afraid to even glance in a mirror because I knew the real reason behind my being pale, and I was afraid I might see how much my appearance might reveal.

I can't remember how I told her. I only remember the haunting look in her eyes as the words came out. I remember her struggling for her breath. And then she crumpled to the floor.

After she came to, she found the strength to pull herself together. She told me she would always love me, and she would stand by me and support me through anything. And then she told me to come here. She told me she had learned to always choose life over wallowing in what is dead, and that is what I should do as well. So, here I am.

******

Officer Warner didn't look me in the eye at first. He just typed a few more notes into his laptop. Even after finishing that task, he continued to look down at his desk for several minutes before looking into my eyes.

"You conspired with your friend, Willie, to kill your father. Is that correct?"

"Yes, but I . . ."

"And the place you planned to do this was underneath the Burnside Bridge, right?"

"Yes, but . . ."

"Then when you walked with your father to that spot under the bridge, you had to know what Willie would do, and yet you didn't act to stop him. That was what happened, wasn't it?"

The tears streamed down my face. "I tried . . . too late."

I could see compassion in the officer's face. "Look, Derek, even if it is true, you didn't kill your father. You didn't strike any of the blows which killed him, but you are still guilty of conspiracy to commit murder. In Oregon that carries a minimum sentence of ten years in prison. If you survive that, and some do not, you will be a thirty-year-old with a record, and finding a job will be extremely difficult. You know that, don't you?"

I lowered my head and nodded.

Even with my head lowered I could feel the officer staring at me. It was several minutes before he spoke again. "I knew the Peacemaker, you know," he finally said. "I don't know anything about what happened before at the University, but I know what he did on these streets. He did a lot of good. Are you still not wanting to be thought of as his son?"

I lifted my head and looked him in the eye. "Yes, I do want to be thought of as his son now. It's too late, maybe, but I do."

"It's not too late. You know, you look like him."

The tears welled up in my eyes again. I had heard those words before, but now that judgment felt like a crushing pressure on my chest.

"Your father fell further than he ever thought he could when he failed in marriage and in his relationship to you. My bet is that there was a time when he considered giving up, ending the pain of it all. Don't you think?"

I couldn't even nod. I just looked at him.

Officer Warner pressed an intercom button and called for assistance.

"My guess is that you will end up at Oregon State Penitentiary down in Salem," he said. "A lot of fallen souls down there like you. What do you suppose your father would do inside those walls?"

I'm not sure what Officer Warner meant to say with that question, but it didn't depress me, or bring back my rage. In fact, it gave me an unexpected lift. I started to feel and visualize my father's presence. He stood behind Officer Warner, smiling down on me. He walked beside me to the holding cell. He accompanied me to court, whispering in my ear. And he even went with me to prison, not only giving me comfort, but opening my ears to the hurting souls around me.

You never know what grace is until you discover a love that has been with you all of your life, but which you have scorned and desecrated—a love like that comes to you and sits quietly with you in the night. I had my father back. He never left again.

Oregon State Penitentiary wasn't so bad. There was this one Black dude who reminded me of Willie, only even angrier. I was the sole white guy who he would even talk to. I met five different men who had killed their fathers, and all but one of them felt haunted by it. They envied me when my mom came to visit. Everywhere I found men who had felt driven to their crimes by a rage which had so taken over their life that they didn't even recognize who they had become. And they kept coming, seemingly every week, over 2000 lost souls, cornered into facing themselves by the tall, thick concrete walls. I listened like the Peacemaker and did what I could.

I had just ten years to touch them all.

A Revival

She made the mistake of asking about my dreams. Did I still have something I was reaching for that was better than scrounging around on the streets of Portland, Oregon? Did I still have something that made my heart beat a little faster, that lifted my eyes toward something a little higher? How was this shitty thing called life going for me?

"Fuckin' great," I said. "How goes your slutty life, bitch?"

And she left. Some people can give it out, but they just can't take it. Ya know?

Yeah, I shouldn't have said it, but what can I say now? It's all personal. My dreams are all either dead or in a deep coma. I could have told her that, and she would have had this pitying look on her face and would have gone on some long spiel about how you should never give up on your dreams, and without your dreams real life just ends, and *blah . . . blah . . . blah*! I know all that, but dead is dead!

My dreams were alive once. I was going to be the lead singer in a rock band. I could make a guitar sing, and with drums I could synchronize the heartbeats of a whole assembly of high school souls. The girls loved me then.

In school I dreamed of screaming, partying crowds who longed to get backstage with me; dreamed while teachers droned on, dreamed while others listened, dreamed even while the teacher asked me questions. I suppose I should have listened more.

"Did ya see what happened on American Idol last night?" the idiot asked.

"No, because, you see, when I plug my big screen TV in out here on the street, it shorts out in this fuckin' rain."

"They let ya watch it over at Fred Meyer, ya know," he said, "so ya don't have to be such a sarcastic shithead!"

"Yeah, well, I am what I am—it's in my nature," I said. "Besides, don't you know that shit is fuckin' rigged? Why watch some amateurs learn to kiss ass? What do rich corporate TV bastards know of the dreams of a real artist anyway? It's all a crock of shit."

And he left. Some people just have no artistic sense.

I had other dreams, too. I would make my father proud. That one died when my father died. He had been proud of me once. He named me Cole. He said he named me after his favorite childhood nursery rhyme,

"Old King Cole was a merry old soul,
And a merry old soul was he . . ."

I was told that as a child, I was merry; especially merry every time my father or anyone said that rhyme. I would smile and laugh and dance in circles. My smile would make my father smile. He used to say that that was all he wanted from his son—for him to be merry, to live a happy life.

But he lied.

Oh, I'm not sure if he lied to himself, or just to me and everyone else, but I'm sure he lied. My father was a Pentecostal minister, and as long as I was little and got up and danced in church during his sermons—so all the people would say I was full of the Holy Ghost, even at such a young age—then yeah, "merry" was good. But a guy grows up, ya know. Ya hear a different kind of music, and dance to words ya never heard from your father. But I danced, damn it! I was merry.

Somewhere along the way he stopped smiling.

Somewhere along the way I stopped smiling, too. Yeah, you don't smile much when ya sleep out on the street and worry about shadows.

Anyway, my dad is dead. No pleasing him now, but that's okay because there was no pleasing him then either.

I dreamed of marrying Ashley, having kids and being a better father than my dad ever thought of being. Yeah, that dream might not be dead yet, but it's definitely on life support. For a while this dream lived. I thought she would turn me down when I asked her—an unstable rock star wannabe who couldn't hold a real job. But I guess at first, she shared the dream.

I did the old-fashioned, down on my knee bit as we looked at the lights of Portland on a miraculously clear night. The Rose Garden surrounded us, and words which before had always seemed to fail me when said aloud, came out flowing freely. How could she resist?

For a while it was a magnificent dream—our passion sustained us, and underneath the covers of our bed we found our retreat from the cold and hostile world. Nothing could touch us there.

But then, I don't know, it all seemed to change. The child who at first bonded us even more strongly, switched on some kind of responsibility app in her that couldn't be found in me. I wanted to play. You play with children. That's what you do.

It was all forcing me into someone I couldn't be. A musician selling cars that advertised the success of others. A father who felt like a child to his own wife. A dreamer starved of everything but fantasy. I don't know where she found her retreat after that, but I found mine in a bottle.

"Hey, Cole," said the Snake, who was supposed to know me, "what do you hear from your kid these days?"

"I hear what a fucked-up bastard his father is, Snake. Hell, what do you hear from your fried-out brain? Is it still vacationing in fuckin' Iraq?"

"Just concerned, that's all," he said. "No need for friendly fire here."

But he stayed. That's why I like the Snake. He stays.

I did notice, however, that more and more the Snake probed into my past. I think he wanted to find something to fix, something he could rescue me from. That's the way he's been ever since the Peacemaker died, trying to rescue people.

"I just said what I said 'cuz I don't want you to give up on it all, ya know?" said the Snake. "A dude's got to have something he hasn't given up on."

"Not true, Snake. There's a certain peace in giving up. You know there's nothing out there to make ya crash. You're already crashed. That's it! No need to fuckin' worry about it. When you're already flushed down the crapper, who cares about the next person who wants to piss on you?"

He didn't say anything then, but I could tell something was working its way through his short-circuited little brain. Yeah, Iraq had done a number on him. I'm not criticizing my best friend, I mean, ya get that, right? When part of your mind keeps wanting to process all the shit that happened in that godforsaken little war, and another part just wants to put up roadblocks against letting it get out, then hell, you get an information traffic jam that would send Bill Gates to tech support.

"The Riverfront Blues Festival starts tomorrow," he said. "We should go."

"It's the one fuckin' event I look forward to all year long, so yeah, I'm goin'."

The Snake knew that, so I don't know why he thought he had to ask. The Riverfront Blues Festival was held annually as a benefit for the Oregon Food Bank. So, I went because without the Oregon Food Bank, I would probably starve, but also because, well, the music. I still love it. Yeah, there were ways in which it was dangerous for me, because it would wake up my music dreams, and for weeks afterwards I would shiver in fear of the inevitable fall. But it was like a drug. I could never resist.

"I guess they will still let me in," he said.

"I don't know, Snake. Last year you had one of your little episodes and mistook the Blind Boys of Alabama for Sunni militants. I don't think the lead singer appreciated you 'disarming him' of his guitar."

"I'm better now."

"Yeah, but they don't know that."

"Maybe they won't be there."

"Yeah, and besides, they're fuckin' blind. How will they know?"

The Snake was absorbed in thought for a few seconds. "Can they smell me, do ya think?"

"Yeah, maybe, 'cuz I sure can."

The Snake was not amused.

******

I should admit the Snake was not the only one who hoped the Blind Boys of Alabama would not be at the Riverfront Blues Festival. I can't say they weren't good. They were. It's just that their music kept reminding me of my religious childhood, and the really tough thing was the memories weren't that bad. When they sang about "Taking the high road to the Promised Land" my body wanted to get up and do a Holy Ghost dance, and my spirit wanted to believe in hope. That part really scared me. I knew I couldn't afford to hope.

So, as we made our way through the gate, both of us were looking around nervously, and of course I figured we were nervous about the same thing.

"Do ya think they're here?"

"Who?" he said. "Who are ya talkin' about?"

He had said it with such genuine confusion that I rolled my eyes.

"Who the hell do ya think? The fuckin' Blind Boys of Alabama! God, man, are you off your meds again? Do I have to put out an alert for everyone to hide their guitars?"

He laughed and seemed strangely relieved. "Oh . . . no, I'm okay. I'm not worried about them. But just to be safe, maybe we should make our way to the blues stage. The gospel bands generally play over at the Miller Stage."

I should have suspected something right then. The Snake really liked gospel; while normally showing indifference to the harder rock-style blues we would encounter at the blues stage. But maybe I was just too relieved to be headed in that musical direction.

"Yeah, that's what I'm talkin' about!" I said. "I can dust off the old air guitar and ya won't have to talk to me for hours, 'cuz I will be in my groove!"

"As much as the idea of not talking to you for hours might normally appeal to me," said the Snake, "I'm still not adjusted to the idea of being alone with my own non-hallucinated thoughts. Some real talking might not be such a bad thing."

He was telling me he was glad I was around. Go figure.

On that Fourth of July weekend, the sun had broken free of weeks of cloud cover, and its warmth invigorated our steps. So did the guitar riffs of Eric Burdon and the Animals, music now emanating from the "First Tech Blues Stage," which we approached.

My body gyrated as I strummed the air and wailed, "Oh! Oh, no! Don't bring me down!" The song came out well before my time, but it spoke to me across time, crying out against all the so-called teachers and all the proper girls and all the street suits strolling past with their noses in the air. With each step I took, I separated myself in my mind from the crowd around me and merged with the band on stage. "I'm beggin' ya' darling! Oh! Oh, no! Don't bring me down!"

In my mind I was now singing the song to Ashley before she left me. At first, she was ready to bolt, but as I poured my heart out in the song and my eye caught hers, she hesitated. I knew this hesitation came because she could see my soul through my eyes and hear my heart through my singing. She could hear how sorry I felt for failing her. She could see how much I needed her to stay. She could hear the deep pain inside of this man she once said she loved. She could see the tears in my eyes—tears that for some reason I had not been able to shed when she had driven off in her car that day with my son in the back seat, the flesh and blood that issued from our love leaving my life perhaps forever. Now, however, in my mind she could finally see that I loved her.

All of a sudden, I realized the music had stopped. I became aware of one more thing: I realized that I had avoided the gospel music in order to avoid dreaming and then crashing; but now I floated high, with the rocky, hardened ground now far beneath my feet, and I started to fall.

I have learned that when my dreams start to crash, the Snake is a good person to have around. I'm not exactly sure why. Maybe it's because he's had his own share of crashing dreams; or maybe it's because when mine crash, he's still there. Giving me a hard time, of course, but there.

So, I looked for the Snake and at first could not find him anywhere, which did make me panic just a little bit. I didn't recognize anyone around me, and several people looked at me as if they were trying to decide whether to call security, based on my appearance alone. Yeah, well, I hadn't shaved in three days; I hadn't changed my clothes in four; there was a scar on my forehead from where some guy had tried to mug me; and my eyes were bloodshot as hell from sleeping on the street with one eye open. Had I looked in the mirror, *I* would have called security.

I must have been drifting toward the stage during the music, so I turned around and picked my way through the crowd. Sure enough, I saw the Snake back about twenty yards from where I was now situated. He stood up, looking back at the gate, waving to someone, but my eyes were no longer good enough to tell who it might be.

"Tryin' to get someone to fuckin' rescue you from me, Snake?" I said, "You can give up on that shit, 'cuz ain't nobody goin' to do it."

The Snake seemed a little surprised by my voice, but when he turned around, he recovered quickly. "Yeah, you caught me. I saw them on the web: shitheadrescuesRus.com. And they guarantee their work!"

I stared at him blankly.

"I'm KIDDING! Man, what's wrong with you?"

I sat down, and he joined me on the ground.

He studied my face for a few seconds. "Okay, when I lost you in the audience your eyes had a spark I hadn't seen in a while; but now the fire has gone out and you're hittin' me with the old street thug language, so what's going on?"

"What do you mean, 'what's goin' on?'" I shot back. "This is who I fuckin' am, and you of all people should know it! If you don't fuckin' like it, you should just leave me here and sit somewhere else!"

"I GOT NOWHERE ELSE TO GO!" he shouted with this overly dramatic look on his face. Then he grinned at me for a few seconds. "Come on now, Cole. I know you've seen *An Officer and a Gentleman* a couple of hundred times. Me, I watched it every day before I enlisted. You have to recognize that line!"

I looked over at a couple of young girls who were staring at us after the Snake's outburst, and I flipped them the bird.

"Okay, I recognize the line—from back when I actually had a fuckin' TV set."

"Ah, yes, a 'fuckin'' TV set," the Snake said, while rubbing his chin philosophically—"that must be one tuned to all the porno channels."

I didn't even smile.

"Come on, Cole, ease up a little, will ya? I mean, even you've got to get tired of the 'f' word sometimes."

I shook my head. "I'll tell ya what I get tired of—rising up and crashing, rising up and crashing. And I know that every time I crash, you're there for me, and don't think I don't appreciate it—but, damn it, Snake! I'm a thirty-eight-year-old shithead going nowhere, and I get my psychiatric care from someone called 'the Snake' who has fuckin' PTSD! How do you think that feels?"

The Snake's nostrils flared and his eyes flashed. "Not as bad as *being* someone with PTSD, let me guarantee you!—and that's *recovering from* PTSD, by the way. Don't think that's easy."

I had just seen the Snake come as close as he had ever come to getting angry at me. And yeah, I deserved it. He recovered and regrouped while I rehashed and relived.

He even recovered quickly from my pissy attitude. He looked back behind us and when his eyes returned to meet mine, they once again were lit by a smile.

"Ya know, sometimes ya just get another chance, whether ya want it or not," he said.

Yeah, I remember he definitely said that. I might not have remembered had it not been for what happened next. He got up and walked quickly toward the food kiosks behind us, but I learned quickly this wasn't about food. As my eyes followed his unexplained departure, they caught a familiar figure coming towards me. My heart did a flip and then accelerated into overdrive, but my head refused to recognize the person until she had come up and sat down in the space which the Snake had vacated. Even then she didn't speak to me. She just focused forward toward the stage where Eric Burdon and the Animals launched into another song.

"We Gotta Get Out of this Place!" blared over the loudspeakers, but at the time I paid little attention because my eyes were transfixed by the beauty of the face now next to mine. I visually caressed the soft contours of cheeks I had kissed so many times before. My eyes reached out to take in the full lips I had longed to rejoin, but which I knew I dare not touch. Then my right hand, moving of its own accord, moving against the frightened cries of my churning memory, floated across the gap between us to rest gently on hers.

Ashley looked my way, and I saw a lone tear escape from her left eye.

"You look so real," I whispered, as if afraid to spook a deer stopping by a mountain stream.

"Yeah, you too." She moved a little closer as she spoke, perhaps to adjust for the music which, strangely enough, I no longer heard.

Suddenly I was aware of my soul rising up within me to stage a jail break, but the warden in my heart quickly clamped down and screamed an angry scream:

"What the fuck do you think you're doing, coming—"

Ashley immediately put one gentle finger on my mouth. "No . . . no . . . no." She underlined the word by shutting her eyes and slowly shaking her head. When she could tell she had stopped the potentially lethal flow of words, she withdrew her finger and kissed me softly on my lips. Then she looked into my eyes.

"I know you're scared, Cole. I am, too. But I'm not going to let either of our fears ruin what will be our last chance with each other. Yes, you can push me away with your brutal language. But I'm asking you not to."

Even as she spoke, every word that sought to jump forth from my mouth was what I knew to be an attack word. I opened my mouth to speak several times, but I did not have the breath to expel even one syllable.

"You'll have to enter a recovery program, Cole. You'll have to get a job. Maybe we can even start going to church again. And damn it, Cole, there's a thirteen-year-old boy out in my car right now who you're going to have to start being a father to again!" She put her hands gently on my cheeks. "You can do this, Cole. I know you can! Suck it up and just say 'Yes'!"

I shivered. The desired word would not come, but a different phrase did come to my lips. "If I don't get to one of those outhouses, I'm going to piss my pants!"

Ashley knew me well enough, she didn't so much as roll her eyes. We stood up together and walked back to the row of porta-potties lined up near the entry to the festival. In spite of my genuine need, I took my time walking, because for the life of me, I did not know what my next step would be after relieving myself.

God, how I wished for the ability to piss out ALL the poisons inside me.

******

It seemed like hours had gone by. I'm sure it couldn't have been. Must have been just maybe five minutes. Anyway, it seemed like a long time before I got up the nerve to leave the porta-potty. I knew, of course, what waited for me.

The first person I saw was the Snake. How I hated him! He knew what this would do to me, and yet he had done it anyway. I felt like walking over and beating the shit outta him.

Then I saw Ashley. On this beautiful, sunny Portland day she stood at the edge of shadows. Were they really just shadows created by the surrounding kiosks?

"Are you going to stand over there all day?" asked Ashley. "You know we're not coming to you, right? You've got to make the move."

My body took several steps in their direction, while my mind fled back toward the stage. So that's why it took me a little while before I realized I was being asked questions.

"Cole!"

"What?"

"I've been talking to you, Cole!" said Ashley. "Please! Keep your head with us, okay?"

I stood a few feet from them now, my mind still in a haze. Still, I know I started to say words.

"That song . . . uh . . . the song they were singing a little while ago . . . I can't remember . . ."

"You can't remember a song?" asked the Snake.

"No, no. I mean, how does that chorus end? I can't remember how it ends."

"What song are you talking about, honey?" That was Ashley, not the Snake.

"On the stage. That last song."

"'We Gotta Get out of this Place'?"

"Yeah, that one! I can't remember! I should remember because my dad used to play it all the time. One of the few nonreligious songs he still played. He said it had been a kind of theme song for his high school graduating class. I know it! Why can't I remember the end of the fu- . . ." I stopped myself mid-swear. "Why can't I remember the end of the chorus?"

Ashley was baffled, but the Snake came to my rescue. He took out his own air guitar and belted out the answer I was looking for. The Snake sang like Bob Dylan going through puberty, but the words came forth from him in a passion:

"*We gotta get out of this place*
If it's the last thing we ever do
We gotta get out of this place
Girl, there's a better life
For me and you."

I looked at Ashley, and I swear my heart stopped.

Tears overflowed her eyes as she looked up at me.

I had been betrayed by my own confused memory—and by God as well. I had given God's Gospel music the slip and he had hit me with Eric Burdon. That sly old bird! The very words I had forgotten and had searched for were the words which lured me to dream again. Still, as I looked into Ashley's eyes, all my fears dissolved in their warm liquidity.

And right there I did a little Holy Ghost dance.

"For me and you," she whispered after I had finished.

The world around me simply disappeared. A smile had come to my face. I reached out and took hold of her hand.

"For me and you!"

Also by Keith Madsen

FICTION:

Searching for Eden, Second Edition, (Edmond, OK: Quill Hawk Publishing, 2021) ISBN: 978-1-7372037-7-3. When Evan Jordan's 14-year-old daughter dies of cancer, he goes on a quest to find a place where children don't die, and where life is still good. His dying daughter had expressed an interest in the Garden of Eden. Could it be that such a place still exists? He goes searching for that garden, hoping thereby to rediscover the goodness and innocence he lost with his young daughter's death.

The Sons and Daughters of Toussaint (Edmond, OK: Quill Hawk Publishing, 2023) ISBN: 979-8-9875646-9-1. In this commercial fiction novel with a historical backdrop, Isaac Breda seeks to renew the revolution of his famous forefather, Toussaint Louverture. He is discouraged that a revolution that had cost so much now has so little to show for it, and he determines to make Haiti's freedom real. He enlists his friends, including his beautiful girlfriend, Marie-Noelle. In pursuing this quest, they are inspired by the words of Margaret Meade: "Never doubt that a small group of thoughtful, committed citizens can change the world; indeed, it's the only thing that ever has."

The Bridles of Armageddon, Second Edition, (Edmond, OK: Quill Hawk Publishing, 2023) ISBN: 979-8-9850905-7-4. In this action/adventure thriller, the nation's cultural war turns bloody as a right-wing demagogue believes he is God's agent to start the Battle of Armageddon. The results quickly move beyond terrorism to full-scale war. Drew Covington, a nationally syndicated conservative columnist, and Shawna Forester, a liberal schoolteacher, are caught up in the resulting struggle and must decide where they stand. Must their nation and world be rent apart to bring heaven to earth?

NON-FICTION:

American Heresies: Reclaiming the Faith of Christ from Donald Trump (East Wenatchee, WA: keiththewriterguy, 2025) ISBN: 979-8-218-62355-5. Donald Trump's upside-down Bible style of Christianity seeks to say we can favor the rich over the poor, disregard the needs of all people who are not white American, lie until the cows come home, abuse women and pretend that "the Good News" is a commodity for the profit of the wealthy few. Is that what Jesus came into this world to teach us? In this book, Keith Madsen uses over 100 Bible passages along with quotations from Christian leaders present and past to show why this Christian attempt to validate Trump and his policies is nothing less than heresy. He is bold to say…***"…whatever is presented as Christian that is not Good News for all people is heresy!"***

About the Author

Keith Madsen retired from pastoral ministry in 2016 but is definitely not retired from life. Currently, he serves as a hospital chaplain in Wenatchee, Washington. He has taken five trips to Haiti, working alongside Haitian workers as well as a mission team from the U.S. to help build a new elementary school. Madsen has also published short stories in *Mobius: The Journal of Social Change, Talking River, Short Story America,* and *Adelaide.* He is an active member of an author's cooperative, *TellTale Authors.* Keith lives in East Wenatchee, Washington, with his wife, Cathy.

www.ingramcontent.com/pod-product-compliance
Lightning Source LLC
Chambersburg PA
CBHW030544310726
48979CB00010B/2025/J

* 9 7 8 1 9 6 5 1 4 2 4 8 6 *